TERROR IN THE SUN

Brucena looked up, and, as she did so, Iain Huntley's lips took possession and held her captive.

For a moment she felt nothing, not even surprise. But then as the man's arms tightened, her lips were suddenly soft beneath the insistence of his. Something warm and infinitely marvellous crept up her body. It was so perfect, so unlike anything she had ever felt or known before.

Iain Huntley raised his head and said in a voice it was hard to recognize:

"My darling! My sweet! I have adored you for so long . . ."

"I . . . love you," Brucena whispered and her voice quivered, "but I had not . . . realized it was . . . love."

Suddenly Iain was kissing her again, kissing her with long, slow passionate kisses, kisses that seemed to draw her very heart from her body and make it his . . .

Bantam Books by Barbara Cartland
Ask your bookseller for the books you have missed

Barbara Cartland's Library of Love series

Terror
in the
Sun

Barbara Cartland

BANTAM BOOKS · MOSCOW · TORONTO · NEW YORK ·

TERROR IN THE SUN
A Bantam Book / October 1979

ISBN 0-553-13126-5

Published simultaneously in the United States and Canada

Bantam Books are published by Bantam Books, Inc. Its trademark, consisting of the words "Bantam Books" and the por-
trayal of a bantam, is Registered in U.S. Patent and Trademark
Office and in other countries. Marca Registrada. Bantam
Books, Inc., 666 Fifth Avenue, New York, New York 10019.

PRINTED IN THE UNITED STATES OF AMERICA

Author's Note

On New Year's Day 1833 William Sleeman set out on an official tour of his territories, carried in a palanquin proceeded by an elephant and escorted, as usual, by Sepoys and Cavalry.

With him was Amelie, his wife, and on the sixth day out from Saugor she was seized with labour-pains. They pitched camp in a grove of lime and pepper trees, a place which for generations had been notorious as a *bele*—a haunt of Thugs. There the Sleemans' son was born.

Several years later, William Sleeman was appointed Resident at Lucknow. One of the heroes of the British Administration in India, he died in 1853, a Major-General, Resident at the Court of Oudh; he was also recommended for a Knighthood, which was awarded posthumously.

By 1841 Thuggee had been virtually exterminated, although the Office of Superintendent survived until 1904.

Chapter One

1832

"Is it your pleasure, Sahib Major, that the train be permitted to leave?"

The Indian guard spoke with respect. At the same time as he spoke, he glanced over his shoulder at the turmoil that was taking place on the platform.

A scene of confusion had heralded the arrival of the train, which, just introduced in India, was thought to be a terrifying fire-breathing dragon.

Indians in dhotis, saris, swathed torn rags, and loin-cloths were all in a state of noisy frenzy. Hawkers shouting in hollow voices were peeping through the windows of the packed carriages with pleading eyes, offering chapattis, coloured sweetmeats, and orange and crimson drinks.

Priests in yellow robes, soldiers in scarlet uniforms, and porters with huge loads hustled against one another.

There were the inevitable passionate good-byes and shouted instructions to those who were leaving from those who believed they were risking their lives in travelling in this dangerous monster.

But Major Iain Huntley was watching a number of men who were clustered together behind a pile

1

of baggage and he was certain that they were there
for no other reason than to cause trouble.

Even as the guard moved away from his side,
unfurling his red flag as he did so, pandemonium
broke out.

The Indians began to rush forward, shouting
and screaming and waving their arms or sticks. Almost like magic, a number of soldiers appeared
with muskets, moving quickly into place to hold back
the threatening throng.

There were few of them compared to the rioters
who, intent on making a nuisance of themselves,
were jumping over, or pushing to one side, the
families who, not travelling on this particular train,
were sitting or sleeping on the platform beside their
cherished possessions, which consisted mostly of
fragile parcels tied up with string. Each group
seemed to contain numerous children besides an inevitable goat or two.

The onslaught from behind took them by surprise and they were rolling over, screaming as they
did so, the shrieks of their children and bleating of
their animals adding to the general tumult.

Chapattis flew in every direction, the heavy
glasses containing the coloured drinks were smashed,
and a goat got loose and rushed down the platform,
with its owner in hot pursuit.

Major Huntley thought with relief that the soldiers would be able to control everything once the
train had left, and he moved without hurrying
toward his own compartment, where he could see his
servant standing by the open door, awaiting him.

The wheels were beginning to turn and the
steam and the hiss of the engine transcended every
other noise, while the mere size of the British-
manufactured locomotive seemed to dwarf everything
else.

Then just as he had almost reached his carriage,
to Major Huntley's surprise, the next door was flung

open and a woman in white stepped out onto the platform.

He saw immediately, with the quickness of a man who is used to the unexpected, that she was intending to rescue a baby who, knocked over by the rioters, was lying unattended on the platform, in imminent danger of being trodden underfoot.

Small though it was, little more than a bundle of rags, it was screaming ferociously.

One second before her outstretched arms could pick it up, Major Huntley swung the woman round and pushed her back into the carriage.

By this time the train was moving with a steadily increasing pace, and since there was no time to reach his own carriage, he swung himself in after her, closing the door behind him.

He looked back to see a forest of shaking fists and hear the yells of the rioters, which sounded like a pack of jackals deprived of their prey.

As the wheels quickened and the station platform was left behind, Major Huntley turned to look at the woman he had unceremoniously propelled back into her carriage.

To his surprise, she was young and exceptionally pretty.

She had discarded her hat and her dark hair curled about a white forehead, while her eyes, large, dark, and flecked with gold, regarded him angrily.

"Thanks to your interference," she said sharply, "that baby will doubtless be killed!"

"What are you doing here and who are you?" he asked bluntly.

He sat down as he spoke and looked round him with an incredulous air, as if he had expected to find that there was someone else accompanying her in the carriage.

He saw, however, that it was empty, and, turning to look at the woman, before she could answer his first question, he asked:

"Who put you on this train? They had no right to do so."

"I should have thought that anyone can travel on a train as long as they can afford the ticket!"

"Not on this particular train, which is going to Saugor."

"Yes, I know, and that is where I wish to go."

"To Saugor?"

The girl, for she was little more, drew herself up.

"I suppose," she asked after a moment, "that you have some authority to question me?"

"I have every authority," Major Huntley said firmly. "I gave orders that no Europeans were to travel to Saugor, which is at the moment a forbidden area."

"Why?"

The question seemed to demand an answer, but he replied somewhat evasively:

"Official reasons of administration; but you have not answered my question."

He guessed, as he spoke, that she had no intention of doing so, and in a more restrained tone he said:

"Perhaps we should introduce ourselves. I am Iain Huntley, and as you can no doubt see from my uniform, I am in the Bengal Lancers, but at the moment on special duties in this area."

Major Huntley finished speaking and waited for a reply.

As he did so, he thought the girl he was speaking to was far too pretty and too young to be travelling alone in any part of India, and certainly not in this particular district at this particular moment.

There was a studied pause, as if she resented having to give him any information. Then as if she thought there was no point in being difficult, she said with obvious reluctance:

"My name if Brucena Nairn."

"And you are travelling to Saugor?"

"Yes."

"May I ask why?"

"I am staying with friends."

"I am not being unnecessarily curious," Major Huntley said, "but I would like to know their names."

Again he had the feeling that she would like to defy him and tell him to mind his own business.

She was still angry—he could see that in her eyes, which he thought now were very expressive and seemed, although they were dark, somehow to be filled with the sunshine that in a few hours would turn the plains outside into an inferno of dry heat.

"I am staying," she said at length in a low, musical voice, "with Captain and Mrs. Sleeman."

Major Huntley stared at her incredulously.

"With the Sleemans?" he questioned. "Is that possible?"

"Does it sound to you so very improbable?" Brucena Nairn enquired.

"I cannot believe that William Sleeman could be expecting a guest like you without telling me of her arrival and making proper arrangements for her reception."

Brucena Nairn shrugged her shoulders.

"If that is what you think, there is no reason for me to say any more."

Her small chin went up defiantly and she deliberately stared out the window as though the conversation was at an end.

Almost in spite of himself, Iain Huntley found himself smiling.

There was, he thought, something amusing in the antagonism of this small creature who had no right to be on the train, let alone arguing with him about it.

He thought it wise to be conciliatory.

"I must apologise, Miss Nairn," he said, "but quite frankly, you have taken me by surprise. For

the last week Saugor has been out-of-bounds to all
Europeans. As you saw just now on the station, there
has been a certain amount of trouble, and if you
had been left behind you might have found yourself
in a very unpleasant situation."

"What are they rioting about?" Brucena Nairn
enquired.

"There is usually trouble at this time of the year,"
Major Huntley replied evasively. "But I still cannot
understand why Captain Sleeman did not tell me
that he was expecting you."

As he spoke, he saw, to his surprise, a faint
colour come into the cheeks of the girl opposite
him, and for a moment her eyes flickered.

"He and Mrs. Sleeman really are expecting you?"
he questioned in a different tone.

There was a slight pause before Brucena Nairn
said in a low voice:

"I . . . hope so."

"You hope so!" Major Huntley repeated. "I
should be grateful if you would explain to me exactly
what has happened, and why you are here."

"There is no reason . . ." Brucena began.

Then her eyes met Major Huntley's and almost
against her will she found herself capitulating.

There was something about him, she thought,
that was very authoritative, and she resented it, and
yet at the same time she did not feel she could go
on defying him.

"It is like . . . this," she said after a moment.
"Captain Sleeman is my cousin."

"So he suggested you should come and stay with
him in India?" Major Huntley interposed, as if he
was beginning to understand what had happened.

"N-not . . . exactly."

The words were spoken hesitantly, and he looked
at Brucena Nairn sharply before he asked:

"What do you mean by that?"

"His wife, Mrs. Sleeman, wrote to me asking if

I would find her a...child's Nanny. She is...
expecting a...baby next year."

There was a faint colour in Brucena's cheeks,
as if she was embarrassed to speak of anything so
intimate, and Major Huntley said quickly:

"Yes, yes. I am aware of that."

"I tried everywhere to find a respectable woman who would go to India, but they all refused."

As she spoke, Brucena was thinking that it had
been an impossible task to convince the Scottish girls
in Inverness-shire that they would find India a
desirable place in which to work.

It was not only they who were reluctant but
also their mothers.

"Ah'm no having ma lassie consortin' with the
heathens," they said over and over again. "She'll stay
here, where I can keep ma eye on her."

"But you must see that it would be quite an
adventure as well as being an education," Brucena
had pleaded, only to be answered by one straight-
backed Scot:

"Ma bairn is no having that sort o' adventure
at her age. If it sounds so attractive to ye, Miss
Brucena, why do ye no go yersel'?"

It was that answer that had put the idea into
Brucena's head in the first place.

At the time she had just laughed, but later,
when her task of finding a Nanny for Cousin Amelie
had proved more and more impossible, she had begun to feel as if India beckoned her and she would
be foolish to refuse the invitation.

She had not been happy at home ever since
she had been old enough to realise that she was a
desperate disappointment to her father because he
had wanted a son.

General Nairn had only two interests in life—
his Regiment and the continuation of the Nairn
family.

His greatest joy was opening the books in which

he could follow the history of the Nairns all down the ages and prove that, if nothing else, they were ferocious fighters.

Brucena used to think that ever since he was a boy himself he had dreamt of the day when he would have one or more sons by his side to fight with him and to add trophies of the wars in which they took part to those which already hung on the walls of Nairn Castle.

"I am a failure to Papa," she had told herself before she was nine years old.

In the years that followed she began to realise how much he resented her because she had disappointed his greatest ambition by being a girl instead of a boy.

If she had not been reminded of it in other ways, she could remember it whenever she heard her name.

"Bruce" was a family name of the Nairns and her father had had her christened "Brucena" almost as if he defied the gods who had served him a scruvy trick in not providing the son he so ardently desired.

Then two years ago when her mother had died, her father, with almost indecent haste, had seized the opportunity to marry again.

He had chosen a young woman only three years older than his own daughter but who was very different in appearance and might have been described as "good breeding stock."

Sturdy, heavily built, with no pretensions to good looks, Jean had been proud and excited to marry the owner of Nairn Castle, but she had resented her Stepdaughter's appearance from the first moment she had seen her.

It was inevitable that Brucena's beauty and her attractiveness to men would not endear her to any Stepmother, least of all to one who was so young.

The tension that had always existed between her and her father was accentuated quickly and violently where his new wife was concerned. When six months ago Jean had given birth to the much-longed-for son, Brucena had found her position in the Castle untenable.

She was found fault with frequently by her father, she tried to ignore the hatred in her Step-mother's eyes, and she was sure that once the pampered, adored heir could see and think, he would hate her too

'I must get away,' she had thought not once but a thousand times, but she had no idea where to go.

Her Nairn relations not only did not want her but would feel uncomfortable if they offered her a home without being asked to do so by the General.

Although Brucena had never broached the subject to him, she thought her father's pride would never allow him either to ask for or accept favours from his relatives, most of whom he found boring and seldom invited to the Castle.

All that Brucena possessed of her own was three hundred pounds, which had been left her as a legacy by her grandmother.

She had been instructed not to spend it, and she knew that her father thought it would constitute part of her dowry on her marriage and would therefore save him from providing as much as he might otherwise have been obliged.

Now she knew that because it was her own it was a god-send and she could pay her own fare to India.

She debated in her mind for a long time whether she should tell her father what she intended to do, then decided against it.

She had the feeling that although he disliked her, he rather enjoyed having someone to quarrel with and to scold.

She was there, and when things displeased him he could vent his wrath on her in a manner he would have hesitated to use with anyone else.

Suddenly it seemed to Brucena as if everything fell into place as a plan came to her mind, and she really had little difficulty in putting it into operation.

A girl who had been her one friend after she had grown up invited her to accompany her and her parents to Edinburgh.

"Papa and Mama are going to be very busy," she had said to Brucena, "because Papa has to receive all the important people who are coming from the South for an inspection of the troops. As they thought I would find it lonely, they have suggested I ask you to come with me. We can look in the shops, and we might even be asked to a Ball. Anyway, it would be fun to be together."

"Great fun!" Brucena agreed.

She thought her father would make difficulties about her going to Edinburgh, but to her surprise he said he thought it was a good idea as long as she was not away for long.

He made this condition, she thought, merely because he in fact begrudged her any amusement, although not so violently as he would have done a year ago, before he had had an heir—a son to carry on his name.

In fact, Brucena was certain when she left, with only perfunctory good-byes from her father and her Stepmother, that they were really glad to be rid of her for a little while.

That, she thought, exonerated her conscience from any feeling of guilt about what she was to do.

She stayed in Edinburgh for a week, spending her time shopping surreptitiously for the things she thought she would need in India.

She was intelligent enough not to go to a new

country before learning something about it, and it had been hard to find books at home which told her anything she wanted to know.

There was, however, plenty of information about India in the book-shops in Edinburgh, and she soon accumulated quite a small Library which she knew she would have time to read over and over again on the voyage.

She told her friends in Edinburgh that she had to return home as her father was expecting her, and when they reluctantly said good-bye to her, she took a train to London.

This, she thought as she travelled South, was where the real adventure started.

Strangely enough, Brucena was quite confident that she could look after herself and that she would reach India in safety.

Mrs. Sleeman had sent her full instructions as to how the Nanny, when she found one, was to be sent out.

When Brucena had read the closely worded pages inscribed in Cousin Amelie's elegant writing, she thought with a smile that it was rather like despatching a valuable parcel that must not be damaged on the voyage.

She learnt that the P. & O. could provide for everything, and a Chaperone for the young woman would be found amongst the passengers who would be travelling Second-Class.

Cousin Amelie had written:

There will be Missionaries or Christian women of some organization or another traveling to Bombay, but although I am sure they would not accept money for their services, which they would look upon as an act of charity, you must of course provide the woman you are sending with an adequate present to recompense them for their kindness.

In the P. & O. Office Brucena had rather a different story to tell.

"I have to journey to India to stay with relatives," she said, "but unfortunately the lady who was to Chaperone me has been taken ill, and I am wondering if you could find anyone who would be kind enough to look after me on the voyage?"

The official stared at Brucena's pretty face and thought a Chaperone would certainly be needed for such an attractive girl.

There were always officers returning from leave, and dealing with ship-board romances was what every Purser found to be one of his less-arduous duties.

Sometimes, however, they could be traumatic when the passengers were cooped up for so long with one another and there was no chance of getting away.

He had, however, as Mrs. Sleeman had expected, been only too willing to oblige.

"I think I have exactly the lady you need, Miss Nairn," he said. "Canon Grant and his wife are returning to Bombay and I am certain Mrs. Grant would be only too willing to oblige, when I explain the circumstances."

"It would be very kind of you to do so," Brucena said.

She had known by the expression on the official's face that he would leave no stone unturned to help her.

Mrs. Grant and her husband had, for that matter, proved a worthy but extremely dull couple. Officially they had provided Brucena with an umbrella of respectability, but they had not interfered with her and she was able to spend a great deal of time reading.

She also enjoyed the sports on board ship and in the evening found herself the centre of attraction

amongst the men who wished to dance with her,
much to the disgust of other young women aboard.

It had in fact been the first time in her life
when she had felt free, without being continually
found fault with, as she had been at home.

It was a joy to be able to express an opinion
without being slapped down, and a greater joy than
she could ever put into words to know that whatever
her father felt about her deceiving him, he could do
nothing about it.

She had spent what seemed to her an astronom-
ical amount of money on her fare and her clothes,
but she still had some left.

Now that she had taken the plunge and had
left home, she knew in her heart that she would
never go back, and if the Sleemans did not want
her she would find somewhere else to work.

She had cabled them before the ship sailed,
saying:

Have found person you require. Details follow.
Love, Brucena

She deliberately did not state the date of her
arrival or explain that she herself was coming instead of the Nanny Cousin Amelie had asked for.

This was only a precaution because she felt
that perhaps they would not want her and would
take steps to send her home when she reached Bombay.

"They will think," she told herself, "that the
Nanny is coming in a month or so and that the
letter, which I have no intention of writing, will
explain who she is and why I think her suitable."

She thought it over and knew that when she
arrived, ready to do anything that was required of
her, the Sleemans would find it extremely difficult
to make her go home.

"At least they will have to keep me for a little time," Brucena argued with herself.

At the same time, in spite of her reassurance to herself that she would be a far better Nanny than any raw Scots girl, she could not help feeling that she was rather imposing herself on people who might not want her.

Cousin William had always been very pleasant to her.

She remembered that as a child, when he had come to stay at the Castle she had thought him slightly awe-inspiring because he was so clever.

Auburn-haired, blue-eyed, and with a fine large forehead, she had learnt on his second visit several years later, that he spoke Arabic, Persian, and Urdu.

He was Cornish as her mother had been and their families had been neighbours for centuries.

Because of his intelligence he had in his thirties been seconded from his Regiment to Civil Administration, and General Nairn had been impressed by the fact that he had become a Magistrate and a District Officer in Central India much earlier than most other men of his age.

It was three years ago, in 1830, that a letter from Captain Sleeman to the General brought the news that he had been appointed by the new Governor-General, Lord William Bentinck, to a very important position.

"He is the right man for the job," the General had thundered as he read the letter at breakfast.

"What is the job, Papa?" Brucena enquired.

"His title is Superintendent for the Suppression of Thuggee," the General replied, "but you would not understand about that."

He spoke disparagingly, not only as a man who thinks that a woman's intellect does not extend beyond the kitchen or the Nursery, but also because he disliked Brucena's curiosity, which made her ask him questions that he would have welcomed from a boy rather than a girl.

"I have read about the Thugs, Papa," Brucena had replied. "They are a secret society who worship Kali and believe it is their sacred right to strangle people."

"You really should not know about such things," the General said disagreeably, "but William will soon have the abomination under control."

"How will he do that?" Brucena enquired.

"He has been given fifty mounted irregulars and forty Sepoy infantry-men," the General snapped. "It should be enough. It is a job I would have liked myself, when I was younger."

There were a hundred questions Brucena had wanted to ask, but her father had walked from the room, taking William Sleeman's letter with him, and she knew it would be hopeless.

Instead, she tried to find out everything she could about Thuggee, but she had not been very successful, and even in Edinburgh the books she could buy told her very little more than she knew already.

Now as Major Huntley sat regarding her with what she thought was a suspicious look in his eyes, she said:

"My cousin asked me to send his wife a Nanny, but as I could not find the sort of person they required, I . . . came myself."

Major Huntley smiled.

"Without giving them the chance of rejecting you?"

"Yes."

"Now I am beginning to understand. But surely you did not make the voyage from England without having somebody to chaperone you?"

"No. I was chaperoned most efficiently by Canon and Mrs. Grant as far as Bombay. They even found

someone to look after me from there to Bhopal, but
unfortunately she was taken ill at the last moment,
and instead of waiting for them to find someone
else I just came alone."

"I see you are a very enterprising young woman,"
Major Huntley remarked. "At the same time, surely
you are aware that it is unheard of for any woman,
married or unmarried, to travel alone in India?"

"I thought the English had the Indians well
under control," Brucena said provocatively.

"We do our best," Major Huntley replied. "At
the same time, I hardly believe you would travel
in England without either a Chaperone or a maid."

"I can look after myself."

"I rather doubt that. It is certainly something you
must not attempt in this country."

Brucena remembered the screaming, yelling rioters on the station platform. She would not give
Major Huntley the satisfaction of knowing that they
had in fact considerably frightened her, and she
could not bear to wonder what had happened to the
baby.

"Now that you are here," Major Huntley said,
"I can look after you for the rest of your journey,
but I feel you will be somewhat of a surprise to
the Captain."

"Are you working with him?" Brucena enquired.

"I am."

"Then why have you a higher rank than he
has?"

Major Huntley smiled.

"Your cousin is a Civil Servant appointed directly
by the Governor-General. He is Superintendent of a
very large territory, while I am in charge of the
soldiers."

This was a gross understatement, Brucena was
to discover later, of the very special duties he
undertook, but at the time she only smiled.

"As you are working with Cousin William, will

you tell me about the Thuggees? I have been very interested ever since I learnt that Cousin William had this post nearly three years ago, but it is very difficult to find out anything about them."

"Why are you interested?" Major Huntley enquired.

"I am interested in anything about India," Brucena replied. "Actually I was born here, and although I remember nothing about it, I have always wanted to come back."

Major Huntley looked surprised.

"My father served for some years on the Northwest Frontier," Brucena explained. "We left India when I was a year old and although he returned later for several years, my mother and I were left in Scotland."

"And yet the country attracts you?"

"It is strange," Brucena said after a moment, "but ever since I arrived in Bombay I have felt almost as if I have come home."

He looked at her sharply, almost as if he thought she might have been speaking merely for effect.

However, she was not looking at him but at the countryside through which they were passing, thinking that the dry, arid ground, the lost little villages with clumps of trees round a water-hole, the water-buffaloes plodding slowly towards it, were all things she had seen before. Though why she should feel like that she had no idea.

"You asked me about Thuggee," Major Huntley began, and instantly her eyes turned towards him with interest.

"I hope," he went on, "that it is something of which you will learn nothing while you are here. Yet it is in fact important that everyone who lives in this district should be on their guard."

As he spoke, he thought of what he had seen at the Temple of Kali at Bindhachal on the Ganges.

It was a Shrine to which supplicants came at

the end of the rainy season from all over India to propitiate the goddess.

The tracks to the Temple were crowded with bullock-carts, beggars, wandering cows, and barefoot pilgrims.

There was the fragrance of incense and blossom and the smell of dust which swirled round the Temple walls. There was also the stink of death.

Night and day, goats were sacrificed, their blood spilling down the Temple steps, and, combined with their frightened baaing, there were the shrieks of the fanatical devotees who flagellated themselves as they evoked the blessing of the gods.

To Iain Huntley, the blood-goddess, the terrible consort of Shiva the Destroyer, black, furious, and naked, with her bludgeon stuck all about with human skulls, was symbolic of everything he was fighting.

With the protruding tongue and the blood-shot eyes, the haunter of burning ground, in whose heart death and terror festered, was the adored one worshipped by the Thuggs.

This was their holy place and from here the fraternity of stranglers had for hundreds of years gone out to terrorise the travellers of India.

The adherents of the cult had their own rituals, traditions, and hierarchy, and when they strangled strangers on the road they believed that they were killing in Kali's cause.

Wondering how he could possibly explain Thuggee to the young and innocent girl sitting opposite him, Iain Huntley looked back and remembered how it had been the East India Company's traditional policy not to interfere with India's religious customs.

In fact, a blind eye had been turned on the rumours and legends of Thuggee, but the Englishwomen now coming out more frequently from England with their reforming zeal were appalled at the native customs which had hitherto been left to carry on as they had for centuries.

The English were now set to put down the most offensive of these, however ancient or divinely rooted. Human sacrifice and infanticide was forbidden, as was *Suttee*, the practice of the burning of widows.

It was obvious also that something had to be done about the abomination of Bindhachal, the headquarters of the secret society of stranglers.

The cult had not been studied, nor its ramifications looked into very deeply, until Captain William Sleeman, who was in the Company's Bengal Army, had become interested in its ghastly mystery.

He learnt that Thugs worked in absolute secrecy according to strictly enforced rituals.

They were dedicated highway murderers and killed with a well-trained technique of noose-work, knee and grapple, strangling their victims from behind with a yellow silk scarf.

Then they cut the bodies about in ritual gashes, buried them or threw them down wells, burnt any belongings of no value, and carried off the rest.

No trace of the unfortunate travellers was ever left at the scene of the crime.

As in most activities in India, Thuggee was strictly hereditary. A boy was initiated stage by stage into his craft: first as a scout, secondly as a grave-digger, then as an assistant murderer, and finally, if he could show a keen ferocity, as a qualified *blurtote*, or strangler, an aristocrat amongst Thugs.

It was William Sleeman who had found out the pattern and the enormous ramifications of this society, which spread like a poisonous web over the whole of India.

Setting up his Headquarters at Saugor, a drab town set on a forbidding lake in the heart of the Thuggee country, he organised his campaign.

Iain Huntley remembered now that some of the senior officials in the service of Indian Princes were experienced stranglers, and a Sergeant drilling the soldiers of the Ruler of Hockar in the courtyard of His Highness's Palace was another.

Some were the trusted servants of Europeans. Others had spent half a lifetime in the service of the East India Company's armed forces, and one quite recently had been a well-known police informer in other fields of crime.

It was frightening to think that the man you had trusted for years, a soldier who had obeyed your commands, your own servant, might have also taken a sacred oath of Thuggee.

To the Thugs, their work was sacred and they believed their own powers were supernatural.

They were in an occult partnership with their kin of the animal world, the tiger.

One famous strangler had said when questioned:

"Those who escape the tigers fall into the hands of the Thugs, and those who escape the Thugs are devoured by the tigers!"

Perhaps on reflection the tigers were less frightening!

Major Huntley had heard one prisoner admitting that he had committed 931 murders by his own hand.

Another Thuggee gang had three hundred men and boasted of more killings that it seemed possible for any men to achieve even over a number of years.

Iain Huntley knew that the years he had been working with William Sleeman had been the most incredible, the most hair-raising, and at the same time the most exciting years of his life.

How could he explain this to the girl, fresh from England and knowing nothing of India, sitting opposite him?

As if in some way she was aware of what he was thinking, Brucena said:

"I want to understand, and I realise fully that it is a very ambitious idea, but still I have to start somewhere."

"I only regret that in coming to India you have begun with Thuggee," Major Huntley replied.

She smiled. "Perhaps in a way it makes it more interesting. So many people eulogise over the Taj Mahal and the brilliance of the Administration of the East India Company."

There was a touch of sarcasm in her voice which made Major Huntley look at her sharply.

"Our Administration is brilliant in some ways," he said, "but in a land as large and densely populated as India, there is inevitably a great deal left undone."

"That I can well believe," Brucena said, "but I feel in a way it is presumptuous of us to try to change a people whose civilisation goes back long before ours. Who are we to judge whether their beliefs are right or wrong?"

Iain Huntley looked at her in surprise.

This was not the conventional attitude taken by the young women who came to India.

Most were concerned only with the amusement they could find at Government House, in the tea-parties, the polo, the dancing, and the gossipping.

Otherwise they were earnest Missionaries of one persuasion or another, determined that whatever the Indians were doing must be stopped simply because it was different from what they themselves had been told was right or wrong at home.

If there was one thing Iain Huntley really disliked it was an evangelical Imperialism combined with a high moral fervour. He found that those who had made it their life's work were boring and narrow-minded.

He often thought that he preferred the superstition and savagery of India, the widow-burning, the infanticide, to the religious bigotry and tight-lipped, narrow-minded zeal of those who disliked even the beauty of the country because it had a seductive effect upon them.

"I think the first thing you must do," he said aloud, "is to try to understand the Indians as individuals, not as a whole, since each one belongs to a different caste, has a different outlook, and obeys self-imposed rules which no Government, however skilfully administered, can change."

"It would spoil them if we did," Brucena said almost as if she spoke to herself. "That is what I want to understand, what I want to learn about India."

"Why?"

The question was abrupt and she knew that the man asking it suspected her motives as being self-centred inquisitiveness.

"I think the answer to that," she said after a moment, "is that I feel I have so much to learn from India, so much it can give me."

Again Iain Huntley was surprised.

As he was wondering what to say, Brucena went on:

"You said that everyone in India is different. That I understand, where caste is concerned, but surely all of them believe in one thing."

"What is that?"

"Their Karma. All the books I have read speak of 'Karma' as being all-pervading, all-embracing, something to which almost every Indian adheres not only with his mind but with his heart."

Major Huntley contemplated her for some seconds. Then he said:

"You are right, Miss Nairn, of course you are right. I am only surprised that you should come to that conclusion, or that it has been put to you in such a simple form."

"I read it," Brucena said, "but I have a feeling I have always known of it inside me, because it is what I believe myself."

Chapter Two

There was a silence, and Iain Huntley suddenly knew that he could not bear to spoil the idealism and the appreciation of India which he knew this girl felt, by telling her of the sordid and disgusting details of Thuggee.

Because he felt a little bewildered by the revelations she had made about herself, he said in a voice that was harder than he had intended:

"I hope, Miss Nairn, that your ideas of India will not be spoilt by your stay in Saugor."

"I am sure I will find it very interesting whatever it is like," Brucena said, "but I am still waiting for you to tell me about the Thugs."

"That is something I have no intention of doing," he replied, "and I think you will find that your cousins feel as I do: the less said, the better!"

It might have been the way he spoke or perhaps that she was disappointed in not hearing what she wanted to know, but Brucena felt her temper rising.

Ever since she had met this man, she thought, he had been obstructive and difficult, and she still felt that she should have saved the baby, which he had prevented her from doing by pushing her back into the carriage.

He was good-looking, she thought, if one admired that kind of very British appearance, but there was something hard and ruthless about him.

She almost felt sorry for the Thugs because he was one of the people hunting them down and bringing them to justice.

Aloud she said:

"It is quite obvious, Major Huntley, that as far as you are concerned, I am not a welcome guest at Saugor."

"You are not my guest," he replied, "and it is for Captain Sleeman and his wife to welcome you."

It struck Brucena that if they took up the same attitude as the Major, she would have to find herself somewhere else to go, and that might be very difficult.

She looked out the window and knew as the Indian landscape sped past that she wanted, with an almost passionate intensity, to stay in India and discover the country of her birth and learn about its people.

How could she explain to the man sitting opposite her, who she felt was hostile, that India gave her a feeling that Scotland had never been able to do?

There was something warm about it, something which, as she travelled from Bombay she had felt in the brightness of the day and the darkness of the night, she could not put into words.

'It speaks to me,' she thought to herself.

But already she was feeling that she had revealed too much of her inner feelings to Major Huntley and he would not understand.

They sat in silence and because her face was turned away from him he could see only her profile. It was impossible not to admire her small, straight nose, the soft curves of her lips, and her firm little chin.

'She should go back to England where she belongs,' he thought savagely.

Then he told himself that he was being unnecessarily alarmist.

She would be with the Sleemans, and the restricted social life round Saugor would welcome her with open arms.

Like all other girls in India, she would be invited to tennis-parties and doubtless small dinners at which, if there were enough men in attendance, she could dance afterwards.

'She cannot come to much harm if she sticks with that sort of thing,' Iain Huntley thought to himself.

But he had the uncomfortable idea that where Brucena was concerned that would not be enough.

"I expect," he said reflectively after a moment, "that Captain Sleeman will be able to arrange for you to stay with his friends in other parts of India, where you will enjoy seeing far finer scenery and some magnificent Temples which we cannot provide you with in Saugor."

"Are you still trying to be rid of me?" Brucena asked in an amused tone. "You seem to have forgotten, Major, that I am here to work."

"As a Nanny?" he questioned. "I can hardly see you in that role."

"Nevertheless, it is the reason why I have come, and I feel certain that I shall not find it hard to learn what is expected of me."

As she spoke, she thought of what Amelie Sleeman had written in well-phrased French.

Brucena was to learn that because her husband spoke such good French, Amelie had never become very proficient in English.

I do not want a stiff and starchy, stuck-up Nanny who would despise both me and my methods. I just want a Scottish or English girl who will help me to look after my baby and whom I

*can trust not to give him opium to keep him
quiet or some other devil's brew which the Ayahs
use, if one is not watching them.*

It had seemed a simple request at the time,
but now Brucena wondered if perhaps Cousin Amelie
was thinking of something far more sinister than a
lazy Ayah who wanted to keep her child quiet.

The Thugs no doubt loathed Cousin William
for the way in which he was hounding them down
and preventing them from following what to them
was a holy craft.

What would be a better revenge than to strangle
his child or even to abduct it and bring it up in
the cult which he was attempting to destroy?

In one book which Brucena had read she found
that when the Thugs killed a party of travellers and
destroyed all trace of them, they occasionally took
away with them, besides anything valuable, any
especially attractive child.

It was thought that they taught him to be a
Thug or perhaps—far more frightening—sacrificed
him to the goddess Kali.

Brucena felt herself shiver at the thought of
such a thing happening to Cousin Amelie's baby and
told herself that her imagination was running away
with her.

Perhaps Thuggee was not half as bad as it was
made out to be.

The mystery that Major Huntley was making
about it only added to her feeling that it was something she must know more about and not be kept,
as he obviously wished, in happy ignorance of the
truth.

'It is my bad luck,' she thought, 'to have found
a man the very first moment I arrive in India who
has no wish to please me and not only has to obstruct
me in finding out what I wish to know, but who
would like to be rid of me altogether.'

She told herself that she would fight him with every weapon in her power.

She was certain that he would try to convince her cousin that not only was she unsuitable for the job she had come out to do, but that she might also be an added danger in a life that was dangerous enough as it was.

'If Cousin Amelie can put up with it, I can!' Brucena thought.

At the same time, she was apprehensive, and as the train chugged on towards Saugor, she found herself disliking more and more the man sitting opposite her.

* * *

"*C'est impossible!* I cannot believe you are really here!" Amelie Sleeman said later that evening, when they had dined by candlelight.

Punkahs moving overhead made the flames swing backwards and forwards as if they were on board ship.

Brucena smiled at her, then at her cousin.

"I was afraid that you would be angry with me for coming," she replied.

"No, of course we are not," Mrs. Sleeman answered in her attractive, broken English, "but we never dreamed, *mon mari et moi*, when we received your telegram, that you were coming here yourself, instead of sending a Scots girl."

"They were all too frightened to travel to such a heathen land," Brucena answered, "and quite frankly, I was so glad to escape from the Castle. Things have not been very comfortable since Papa remarried."

"That is exactly what I said to my husband," Amelie Sleeman said almost with a note of triumph in her voice. "I said: '*Cette pauvre petite* has had, I am quite certain, a difficult time with a *belle mère* who could never be as pretty as she is!'"

"Well, now you are here, and that is all that matters," William Sleeman said before Brucena could reply, "and I am glad for Amelie's sake that she has a woman to keep her company. She finds it very lonely when I have to be away from home so much."

"That is true," Amelie said, "I should miss you desperately, *mon cher*, wherever we were, but it is somehow worse here when I cannot go anywhere without an escort of soldiers, and I am sure Brucena will find that a bore too."

"She will get used to it," William Sleeman said with a smile, "and let me make this quite clear, Brucena, you are not to go outside the garden without letting the Sergeant in charge of the Sepoys know where you are going, and if it is out of sight of the house, he will send somebody with you."

"There you are!" Amelie exclaimed with an expressive gesture of her hands. "It is just like being one of your prisoners and I sometimes feel *c'est moi* who is locked up and not they."

"I think you would find the gaols at Jubbulpore and Saugor very different from the comfort you enjoy here," William Sleeman said drily, "and at least I do not brand you, my dear."

His wife laughed.

"I suppose I should be thankful for small mercies!" she exclaimed; then, seeing that Brucena did not understand, she said:

"One of the punishments for a convicted Thug is that he is branded on his back and shoulders or even on the eye-lids, which is something they dislike intensely."

"I am not surprised," Brucena said. "The punishment seems very extreme."

"Nothing is too extreme for men who murder for pleasure," William Sleeman said sharply.

There was silence for a moment. Then Brucena said:

"When you have time, Cousin William, I would like you to tell me more about Thuggee. There is very little about it in any of the books on India, and I understand it is one of the most ancient secrets of the country."

"That is true," he agreed, "but I have no wish to talk about it in front of Amelie. In her condition, she should not be worried either physically or mentally with subjects that are unpleasant."

"Yes, of course, I understand," Brucena said quietly.

She had already learnt that Mrs. Sleeman was expecting her baby in the New Year, and at seven months she already looked large and had lost the grace of movement which had been so characteristic of her.

She was the daughter of a sugar-planter from Mauritius and it had seemed an unlikely marriage between two people of such diverse characters, with twenty-one years between their ages. Yet one had only to see the Sleemans together to realise that they were extremely happy.

Because Frenchwomen are very adaptable, Amelie was in fact exactly the right wife for William Sleeman.

"I shall be happy with them," Brucena told herself as she went to bed that night in the small room that was next to the already prepared Nursery, which was where the Nanny would have been sleeping.

Outside she could hear the strange sounds of the hoot of an owl, the chirp of a cricket, the flutter of a bat's wings, the barking of pariah dogs, the scuttle of some nocturnal animal in the shrubs, and far away in the distance the sound that she knew was so characteristic of all India—the howl of a pack of jackals.

It was all very exciting, a new world, and yet an old one which she felt she had sprung from and where her roots still lay.

"I am so happy to be back here with you," she whispered in her heart.

*   *   *

It was three days later that Brucena realised that while she had been "digging herself in," as it were, she had not seen Major Huntley.

He had brought her to the large white bungalow on her arrival and handed her over with the air of a man who was not quite certain if he was producing a pleasant or an unpleasant surprise.

Brucena had been well aware that there was work for him to do, because as they had arrived at Saugor station, a Sergeant in charge of a detachment of Sepoys had been waiting to salute him smartly.

As she was annoyed with Major Huntley she did not bother to explain to him that during the long weeks of travelling on board ship she had studied Urdu and after the first few days had found a teacher in the Second Class who for a small sum of money had given her lessons.

The Purser who had arranged it had assured her that the man was well qualified for the job and Brucena had found him not only a proficient teacher but an intelligent person.

At first she had concentrated fiercely on learning the language, determined that she would not arrive in India unable to speak anything but English.

As the weeks went by, she found to her delight that he could also tell her a great deal about his country and the customs of his people.

He even tried to explain to her the caste system and, more important, the religions, which varied from the Buddhists to the Hindus, from the Jains to the Moslems and hundreds of strange and varied sects, all of which had their rituals, their taboos, and their sacred places somewhere in the vast sub-continent.

Some instinct in Brucena warned her to keep

silent on the subject of Thuggee and not to tell her
teacher that she was to stay with their arch-enemy,
Captain William Sleeman.

She had a feeling that if he was aware of her
destination he might not be so forthcoming in teach-
ing her the things she wanted to know.

She could not quite explain why she felt this,
but she had learnt for many years to trust her instinct, which at that moment told her to keep silent
about herself.

Although she realised that there was a great deal
more for her to learn where Indian languages were
concerned, she understood as the Sergeant met them
on the station what Major Huntley said to him.

In a low voice that she was not expected to
overhear, he said in Urdu:

"Is there any trouble?"

"A little, Major Sahib," the Sergeant replied.
"I think tonight we should visit . . ."

Brucena did not catch the last word, but she
understood the rest and was therefore slightly amused
when, turning to her with a deceptive smile, Major
Huntley said:

"I have told the Sergeant to procure a carriage
for you and I will drive with you to your cousin's
bungalow. You will find it quite impressive to be
escorted by a detachment of Cavalry!"

Brucena had certainly not been impressed by
her first sight of the town of Saugor, except that
anything to do with India had a beauty which she
had never seen anywhere else.

It was set on the shore of a large lake and at
one side of it there appeared to be a huge, gloomy,
castellated Castle, which she learnt was the prison.

The Sleeman's bungalow, which was outside the
town, was large but simple and charming, and the
garden was filled with flowers whose colours made
Brucena feel that they gave her a special welcome.

She knew at once that there was no fear of the Sleemans sending her back or not being genuinely glad to see her.

She felt in a way that the surprised but undeniable sincerity with which Amelie kissed her was in fact an impulsive snub to Major Huntley, although they had not met before.

'He may not want me here,' Brucena thought, 'but my cousins do and that is the only thing that matters.'

At the same time, she enjoyed the feeling that she had scored off him and looked forward, with a feeling which she could not quite understand, to further wordy duels, which, however, were not forthcoming.

Because she was curious, she asked Mrs. Sleeman about Major Huntley.

"Why has he not been here?" she enquired. "He gave me the impression that he was Cousin William's 'right-hand-man.' "

"Oh, he is! That is certainly true," Amelie replied, "and William is very pleased with him. He has captured far more Thugs than any of the other officers who the Regiment sent him. In fact, some of them are worse than useless."

"I thought it was rather obvious that Major Huntley liked being an Inquisitor," Brucena said drily.

"He is very brave," Amelie said, "and though none of my husband's other assistants would admit it, I am quite sure that secretly they are frightened. Thugs are very dangerous, and thank God there are fewer of them than there were."

"Which is all due to Cousin William?" Brucena questioned.

"Yes, of course. He has been absolutely wonderful," Amelie enthused. "His prime purpose in life is not only to destroy Thuggee but to discredit it."

She gave a little sigh.

"William has always said that when men fight

for the sake of a cause they are immeasurably stronger and more formidable than when they fight for personal satisfaction or duty."

"I have often heard that," Brucena said.

"It is true," Amelie went on, "and he is beginning to convince the Thugs that our God is greater than their goddess."

"Can he really make them believe that?" Brucena asked curiously.

"He told me last week," Amelie replied, "that a Thug said to him: 'You say that your God is assisting you and that Kali has withdrawn her protection on account of our transgressions. We must have sadly neglected her worship.' "

Brucena, after this conversation, would have liked to talk more with Cousin William, but when he came home in the evening he was often dead tired.

She knew it was because he had worked hard all day not only in hunting down the Thugs but in arguing with them, fighting them with words as well as with weapons, and in the relaxation of his home he had no wish to talk about it any further.

Both she and Amelie had been forbidden to go near the town for the next few days and had been given no reason for the ban.

But by listening to what was said and by skilfully cross-examining the Sergeant of the Sepoys, who spoke good English, Brucena learnt that there had been trouble because six Thugs had been executed, one of them a local hero.

One of his adherents who could not at the moment be arrested on the charge of Thuggee had managed to stir up Indians of other castes into protesting and making trouble.

It was always an easy thing to arrange political unrest in India, and only by very strong methods of repression had the riots been put down.

It had resulted, Brucena learnt, in the gloomy

prison on the lake being filled to capacity and a
great number of other prisoners being confined at
Jubbulpore.

Just when she least expected it, when she was
alone on the verandah, she heard the sound of horses
in the compound and a moment later Major Huntley
was beside her.

He looked hot and a little tired, but he greeted
her politely, then asked:

"I understand the Superintendent is not here.
When are you expecting him back?"

"I have no idea," Brucena replied. "In fact
Amelie before she went to lie down was wondering
why he had not told her when he expected to return."

She saw the frown on Major Huntley's forehead
and asked:

"Is something wrong?"

"No, no. Of course not," he replied so quickly
that she knew he lied.

"Would you like a drink?" she asked.

"Thank you," he answered.

She clapped her hands as she had been taught
to do when she required a servant, and when the
head boy, who was getting on for sixty, appeared,
Major Huntley asked for a glass of lime-juice.

As he sat down on a chair beside Brucena, the
frown vanished from his forehead as he enquired:

"How are you enjoying yourself? Has India disappointed you yet?"

"I find each day more exciting than the last,"
Brucena replied. "But it is a pity that I am so restricted in what I can see and where I can go. In
fact, I am disappointed that your efforts at keeping
the peace are not more successful."

She meant to needle him and thought he would
protest at her insinuations. Instead he merely laughed.

"I am sure you would be wise after your long
journey to rest for a little while," he said. "And let

me tell you, things are almost back to normal. Soon you will be able to go anywhere you want."

"With, of course, an escort," Brucena finished.

"As you say, with an escort," he agreed.

She looked towards the lake, then over the hard-baked earth which stretched away towards the horizon.

"Is this place really as dangerous as you try to make out?" she asked. "I have a feeling that you enjoy making my flesh creep by hinting at unknown horrors while refusing to name them specifically."

"Surely, Miss Nairn, you are not interested in horrors? Besides, at your age you should be thinking of very different things—romance being one of them."

As he spoke, he looked down at the book which was beside her on the seat.

"I believe," he said, "that the current reading amongst the young ladies at Simla is *Wuthering Heights*. Is that what you have here?"

He picked up the book casually, then saw that it was written in Urdu.

"You can hardly tell me that this is of any interest to you."

For some perverse reason which she could not understand, Brucena decided not to tell him the truth.

"No, of course not," she said. "I think Cousin William must have left it there. There is, I regret to tell you, a shortage of books in the house."

"I should be pleased to send to Jubbulpore for anything you require."

"I would not like to put you to any trouble. Besides, if you did, you would have to come here again, instead of ignoring me, as you obviously intended, since my arrival."

"I see that you are looking on me as an enemy," Iain Huntley said in an amused tone.

"Why not?" Brucena retorted. "You made your

feelings very clear on the journey, and there has been no enquiry as to my well-being since my arrival."

He laughed.

"That was certainly very remiss of me," he said, "but you must accept my excuse that I have been extremely busy."

"Chasing Thugs," Brucena asked mischievously, "as if they were foxes to be hunted down by red-faced huntsmen and a pack of hounds?"

"Exactly! That is a very good simile. Unfortunately, in this instance there were too many foxes and not enough hounds."

Brucena was just thinking of something cutting to say when William Sleeman came striding onto the verandah.

"There you are!" he said. "I was told you were here! I have found out where that man has gone."

"You have, Sir!" Iain Huntley exclaimed. "Where?"

"Need you ask?" William Sleeman replied. "To Gwalior, of course."

"I thought that might be where he would hide," Iain Huntley remarked.

"It is what we might have expected," William Sleeman said bitterly. "The place has become a sanctuary for Thugs. A murderer can return there with as much safety as an Englishman to an Inn."

Brucena was listening wide-eyed.

She knew that Gwalior was a neighbouring Province and that an English Resident had been appointed by the Governor-General to advise the Maharajah there as in many other Courts of the independent ruling Princes.

"It is intolerable, but I am not certain what I can do about it," William Sleeman was saying almost beneath his breath.

"There must be something," Major Huntley insisted.

"I wish there were, but Mr. Cavendish has op-
posed me resolutely ever since I came here and has
made my work more difficult than it need have been."

"It is disgraceful!" Iain Huntley exclaimed.

"Are you saying that the Resident is an Englishman who actually approves of the Thugs?" Brucena asked.

Her voice seemed to startle the two men and
she knew they had completely forgotten her existence.

"He would not admit it," William Sleeman
answered after a moment's pause, "but by blocking
my investigations and disallowing my men into the
Province of Gwalior, he has made the place an es-
cape-hole into which any Thug can disappear when
he is hard pressed."

"It seems an incredible situation," Brucena said,
"when the Governor-General has appointed you to
suppress the Thugs."

"It is," William Sleeman said, "but Gwalior or
no Gwalior, I intend to destroy what is the most
dreadful and most extraordinary secret society in the
history of the human race."

His voice had a dedicated note as he spoke and
there was a look in his blue eyes which was that
of a visionary.

* * *

Later that evening they sat round the dinner-
table and entertained not only Major Huntley but
half-a-dozen neighbours.

It seemed hard to believe, Brucena thought, that
outside the civilised comfort of the room with the
cheerful voices and the laughter of the guests rising
on the warm, heavy air, there were men waiting to
murder innocent and unsuspecting travellers and to
glory in their killing.

It was not a subject to be discussed at dinner,
Brucena realised, so she listened to the local gossip

and the stories of how tiresome and stupid the Indian servants were.

She was shown some amusing little knick-knacks that had been purchased from the native bazaar besides some very lovely material that could be used as an English lady's scarf just as well as an Indian sari.

It was all very feminine and frivolous, but she knew that the young men who were present looked at her with a glint in their eyes, and the older ones teased William Sleeman for having produced such an attractive guest without warning them that she was a beauty.

It was all commonplace and uncomplicated, and yet when Brucena went to bed she stood looking out into the night and felt it was all part of the India that was an enigma, a mystery, and at the same time an enchantment.

She had the feeling that the knowledge she craved, everything she wanted to know, was out there but always just out of reach.

It was hidden behind thousands of years of tradition, behind a complexity of rituals and customs that the Europeans could never understand.

And behind all that was the secrecy so deeply ingrained in the minds and hearts of the Indians who would die rather than reveal what to them was sacred.

* * *

Brucena walked through the garden, knowing, as she did so, that only constant watering almost every hour of the day could keep the small patches of grass from withering away in the heat and protect the flowers, planted painstakingly over the years by every occupant of the bungalow, from being lost in a jungle of weeds.

The wild flowers were beautiful; bougainvillaea swarmed in thick profusion over every wall, and creepers of crimson and white blossoms wound their ways round the trunks of trees.

The gardeners fought an unending battle with the shrubs that encroached almost like an octopus on everything near them.

It was all inexpressibly lovely and Brucena felt as if she moved to hidden music that was part of the beauty of the Indian dawn.

Although it was nearing the end of October it was still very hot in the middle of the day, and William Sleeman had advised Brucena to rise as early as possible, when the air was cool and the earth itself felt fresh.

Sometimes he would take her riding with him before breakfast, but this morning he had to go into the town and she decided to walk through the garden carrying a sunshade, which was as yet unopened, to protect her as the sun rose.

It was all so magical, she told herself, and she could never look at the flowers and the countryside without feeling that they had a special message for her that she could not yet fully understand.

She reached the end of the cultivated garden and stood looking over a hibiscus hedge to where a long, dusty road ran over the sandy, unwatered earth towards some trees in the distance.

She had a feeling that if she walked along the road far enough she would find what she was seeking, and yet she was not certain what that was.

She stood looking at it, feeling that it was symbolic of something which she should understand, but for the moment its meaning escaped her.

Then she heard a sound and, looking to the right, saw a party of people camped in the shade of a few scraggy trees.

The bright saris of the women were vivid against the earth, on which nothing could grow until the rains came, and as they were packing up their belongings that they had obviously used during the night, she noticed that the bangles on their wrists flashed and glittered in the morning light.

They were beautiful women and they had a grace that was enviable, Brucena thought, and she knew it was the years of carrying water-vessels on their heads that made them walk as if they were goddesses.

The men were tending some small, spindle-legged horses and an ancient, rather tired donkey.

There were quite a number of them, and there were children too, playing happily on the ground, one with a piece of wood, another with a coloured rag which he tried to make blow out in a non-existent breeze.

Ever since Brucena had arrived in India she had wished that she could draw or paint the beauty of the Indian children.

Never had she imagined that small human beings could be so exquisite in every way.

With their large eyes and their small faces, they had a helpless appeal that tugged at her heart and invariably made her remember the baby she had not been able to save from the rioters on the station platform.

She was watching them when one little boy of perhaps five years old detached himself from the others and came towards her.

He was carrying a flower in his hand and as he reached her he held it up, with a smile on his lips that made her long to catch him up in her arms.

She took the flower from him.

"Thank you," she said in Urdu. "Thank you very much."

She wondered if she had anything to give him in return, and instinctively put her hand into the pocket that was inserted in the seam of her gown.

She thought vaguely that she might give him a handkerchief.

Then as she felt something soft and silky, she

realised it was a ball of silk that she had picked up on the edge of the verandah as she had left the house.

It belonged to Amelie, who was embroidering a robe for her baby in pinks and blues.

"Pink *and* blue?" Brucena had questioned when she saw it.

"I do not mind if it is a boy or a girl," Amelie said, "and therefore I am placating the gods and making them believe I have no preference in the matter."

Brucena laughed as she said:

"I am sure William wants a son. All men do."

She could not help the slight bitterness in her voice as she spoke, remembering how she had suffered all her life because she was a girl instead of the boy her father had wanted so fervently.

"William says," Amelie said softly, "that if it is a girl and it looks like me, he will be so thrilled to have another Frenchwoman to love that he will have no regrets."

"I hope he is speaking the truth," Brucena said, "but I am praying, dearest Cousin Amelie, that you will have a son as your first child."

"I suppose, if I am honest, I would like a boy, for William's sake," Amelie said. "At the same time, it would be fun to have a daughter to talk to, as you and I talk together."

"From all you have said," Brucena said with a smile, "it should be twins."

"Of course," Amelie agreed, "and the blue will be for the boy and the pink for the girl."

She smiled and it seemed to light up her whole face.

"Whatever it is," she said, "it will be mine. My very own, and that is what will matter."

Brucena drew the little ball of pink silk from her pocket.

She hoped Amelie had enough to finish the robe,

but she could not resist the charm of the small boy who had handed her the flower.

She bent over and put the pink ball in his hand.

He looked incredulous, until as his small fingers closed over it and he made a little sound of delight.

Then he pressed it against his chest as if to assure himself that it was real and she really intended it for him.

"For you!" she said in Urdu. "For you to play with."

He gave a cry that was one of rapture, then ran back to the other children, holding it high above his head and shouting:

"Mine! Mine! All mine!"

It was the sheer joy of possession, Brucena thought, and whether it was Amelie or the little boy, what everyone wanted was something that belonged to them exclusively.

'I have nothing! Nothing that is really my own!' she thought, with a sudden excess of self-pity.

She looked at the road winging towards the horizon and told herself that she had something far more important than possessions.

The knowledge she found in everything new was more exciting than a jewel, more valuable than any fortune.

"That is mine," she said to herself defiantly, "and that is something which no-one can take from me!"

*   *   *

William Sleeman came in to lunch in a good humor.

"I thought that as it grows cooler this afternoon," he said to his wife, "you and Brucena might like to come with me for a drive."

"William dearest, what a delightful idea!" his wife replied. "Are you telling me it is now safe?"

"I hope so," her husband answered. "The last

purge, which we brought off against tremendous odds, has proved so effective that I am certain if there are any Thugs left in this vicinity, they are moving out of it as quickly as their legs can carry them."

Brucena listened attentively.

She had the feeling that if she asked questions Cousin William would change the subject.

"You will hardly believe it," he said, "but a man we have been hunting for the last six months has proved to be an Intelligence Agent in the employment of the East India Company!"

"I can hardly believe it!" Amelie exclaimed.

"It is true, and everyone who worked with him swore that they would trust him with their lives, which in fact was exactly what they were doing!"

"How is it possible that they can reach these important posts without anyone being suspicious?" she enquired.

"That is what I ask myself every time we turn over an administrative stone and find a Thug underneath it," her husband answered. "Well, this man is now behind bars, awaiting trial, and I have a feeling that the fact that we have caught him will be an invaluable deterrent to those who thought him inviolate."

Amelie sighed.

"I think what frightens me more than anything is that they believe their magical powers will save them."

"They are beginning to understand that we are stronger than they are," William Sleeman replied, "and not only by main force. As one man said to me: 'At the sound of your drums, sorcerers, witches, and demons take flight. How can Thuggee survive?' "

"How indeed?" Amelie agreed. "At the same time, darling, you must be very careful of yourself. If anything happened to you, the devils and demons would all be back in force."

"Of course they would!" William Sleeman agreed.

"But so far, I believe, God has protected me because, as even the Thugs admit, I am doing His work rather than the devil's."

Later, when the sun had lost a great deal of its strength and the day was beginning to grow cooler, they sat in an open carriage and drove along beside the lake.

Despite the fact that he had said it was safe to go without an escort, Brucena found that a number of Cavalrymen were riding with them, and she came to the conclusion that it was part of the aura of his importance which Cousin William thought was essential to his job.

She was not prepared to quarrel with him about it because she was so excited to see the country.

The little Shrines by the water, the women in their beautifully coloured saris walking with heavy loads on their heads, small boys driving water-buffaloes, a flock of black and white goats—all were irresistibly attractive.

And the lake itself was an enchantment as the evening sun turned it to gold and children from the isolated villages plunged naked and jubilant into the cool water.

This, she thought, was the India she wanted to see, and even the sight of the vultures, flapping their huge wings as they were disturbed from consuming a half-eaten carcass, did not dispel the feeling of magic.

They drove for several miles before William Sleeman ordered the carriage to return, and now they took another route, moving through undulating country with more trees.

As if it was constantly in his thoughts, he pointed out rows of lime and peepul trees and said:

"Those are all places of abomination where wretched travellers, camping in the shadow of them for the night, have felt a Thug knee in the small of their backs, a Thug breathing behind their heads, and the silken cord pulled tight around their necks."

Amelie gave a little cry.

"William, you are frightening me!"

He reached out his hand and took hers.

"I am sorry, my dear, I did not mean to. In fact, I was actually thinking aloud."

It was what Brucena thought he was doing, and she was exceedingly interested in what he had said.

She had learnt that a place of strangulation was called a *bele*, that a *pola* was a secret sign left by one Thug for another, and a *kburak* was the noise made by a pick-axe digging a grave.

Gradually she was compiling a glossary of her own on everything that concerned Thuggee.

She had already learnt, both from Major Huntley and her cousin, that it was a mistake to ask openly for information; it was far better to listen.

They drove on and now they could see in the distance the town of Saugor.

There were people coming out from the town and Brucena looked at them with interest as they were returning home with the empty baskets which had doubtless held vegetables which they had sold in the market.

Then she noticed, before they reached them, two distinguished-looking men wearing turbans and white-sashed dhotis over pantaloons and sandals with curled toes.

They looked more prosperous and certainly better dressed than any other Indians they had passed, and she wondered if they were strangers to this area, perhaps travellers.

She was just about to ask Cousin William what he thought, when she noticed that between the two men was a small boy.

Even as she looked at him she knew that she had seen him before, although most Indian children looked very much alike.

But this boy was different, and she was certain

that he was the little boy to whom she had given
the pink ball of silk early in the morning in exchange
for the flower.

The carriage drew nearer and the men stepped
off the road to let it pass.

She then saw that the child with the little face
and big eyes whom she had admired and who had
smiled at her so beguilingly was crying.

Tears were running down his cheeks and yet he
was making no sound, only crying in dumb misery.

It was the same small boy—she was sure of it.

Then as one man who was holding him by the
hand released him to put his palms together in the
ancient gesture of *nameste* to salute the English
Sahib, she saw that the child still held tightly in his
hand the ball of pink embroidery silk which she had
given him that morning.

Chapter Three

Brucena held her breath. For a moment it seemed as if a thousand questions flashed into her mind.

Then as she knew what she feared, she was aware that she must not speak of it in front of Amelie.

Already she had said she was frightened, and Brucena had known ever since she arrived in Saugor that William Sleeman deliberately avoided speaking of the Thugs in front of his wife.

It was not only because she was pregnant, but also because, like most Englishmen, he believed that ladies should be protected and cosseted against anything that was unpleasant or violent.

There was a chivalry about him which she knew was part of his Cornish ancestry and she remembered that her Cornish grandfather, whom she had loved had had the same principles.

She therefore bit back the suspicions that came to her mind, and at the same time told herself that she was being over-imaginative.

Cousin William had said that after their last purge all the Thugs had left the vicinity; and yet the riots she had seen on her arrival, because six Thugs were to be hanged, had shown her that a great number of people in Saugor sympathised with them

47

or else were too frightened to take up any other
attitude.

A moment later they passed what was obviously
the rest of the group connected with the two distinguished-looking men who were escorting the little
boy.

There were a number of heavily laden pack-
horses, led by men with beards and turbans, all of
whom looked prosperous and well clothed.

There were no women in the party and
Brucena wondered what had happened to those she
had seen that morning in their brilliant saris, and the
children who had been playing with the little boy
who gave her the flower.

In a voice that somehow trembled despite herself, she asked:

"Where are these people . . . coming from?"

"There has been a big market in Saugor today,"
William Sleeman replied. "Farmers from all over the
Province have brought in their vegetables and fruit
for sale, and their women-folk have come with them
to buy pretty saris and more jewellery to hang in
their noses and round their arms."

It was an explanation which did not answer the
questions that Brucena longed to ask.

If there were so many travellers, would there
not be Thugs too who preyed on them?

Thugs who would await their opportunity under
the lime trees through which they were now passing,
then swiftly and silently commit their terrible crimes
to add everything that the victim had bought to the
spoils they already possessed from other murders.

'It could not happen here and in broad daylight,'
she thought to herself.

Yet the face of the little boy with the tears
running down his cheeks filled her thoughts to the
exclusion of all else.

They drove on, and while Amelie chatted away,
Brucena was silent.

She was wondering what Cousin William would say when she told him what she suspected, and she felt a little apprehensive in case he should laugh her to scorn and tell her to forget the Thugs and just enjoy herself as any ordinary English girl would do in her place.

But she knew she would feel that she had betrayed the child who had given her the flower if she did not ask her cousin to investigate.

She thought to herself that the men and their pack-horses would not get so far that the mounted Sepoys could not catch up with them.

The carriage reached the bungalow and as they drove through the banks of flowering shrubs up to the front of it, Brucena saw Major Huntley waiting for them on the steps of the verandah.

As soon as the horses drew to a standstill he hurried down to lean over the door of the carriage and say:

"Lord Rawthorne has called, Sir, with a letter from the Resident of Gwalior."

"Now why should Mr. Cavendish be writing to you, William?" Amelie asked, before he could speak, "and if he has, I am sure it is only to be disagreeable."

"I think we can be certain of that," William Sleeman said with a smile. "But who is Lord Rawthorne?"

"As far as I can ascertain," Iain Huntley replied, "he is making a tour of India and is staying with the Resident at the moment, with letters of introduction from the Governor-General."

"We must certainly make ourselves pleasant to him," Captain Sleeman remarked.

"He arrived rather late, as he had been delayed on the journey," Iain Huntley went on. "I have therefore, in your absence, Sir, suggested that you and Mrs. Sleeman would be delighted if he would stay the night."

"Quite right! Quite right!" William Sleeman approved.

"I have sent his escort to the Barracks, while he and his personal servants will stay in the house."

William Sleeman nodded his approval as he stepped out of the carriage, and Major Huntley then helped Amelie to alight.

There was no need for him to help Brucena.

She was on the ground before he could put out his hand towards her, and she wondered for a moment if she should tell him of her suspicions.

Then she told herself that he would quite certainly disparage anything she might say and also tell her, as he had already done, that she should not concern herself with Thuggee.

She therefore followed Amelie into the Sitting-Room, where she found a tall, dark man of about thirty-six in conversation with Cousin William.

"I am sorry I was not here when you arrived," Captain Sleeman was saying as they entered the room. "I cannot understand why Mr. Cavendish did not let me know of your arrival so that we could have made preparations to entertain you."

"I did not wish to put you to any trouble," Lord Rawthorne replied. "I intended to be here far earlier, and, having made your acquaintance, to push on to Bhopal, where I have some friends. But by the time I arrived it was too late to proceed further."

"We are delighted that you can stay with us," William Sleeman said. "And now may I present you to my wife."

Amelie curtseyed as Lord Rawthorne bowed.

"And my cousin who has recently arrived in India from England," Captain Sleeman went on, "Miss Brucena Nairn."

As he looked at Brucena, Lord Rawthorne almost visibly started.

There was no doubt of the look of admiration that came into his eyes as he appraised her, Brucena thought, very much as a man might appraise a good horse.

There was something about him that she did not like. She thought it was perhaps his arrogance, his very obvious appreciation of his own consequence.

"You are just out from England as I am," he said. "So we have, Miss Nairn, something in common. What do you think of this strange, wild, unusual country?"

"I find it fascinating."

"I too find many fascinating things here," Lord Rawthorne replied, and there was no doubt that he meant it as a compliment.

Later that evening as they sat at dinner, at which Major Huntley had joined them, Brucena thought there was nothing wild about the scene, and except for the Indian servants, they might have been dining conventionally in any country in the world.

Cousin Amelie and she in their best evening-gowns, Cousin William in his gold-braided tunic, and Major Huntley in the red and blue evening-dress of the Bengal Lancers made the small party colourful and very formal.

Lord Rawthorne would have looked somewhat drab in contrast if he had not decorated his stiff shirt-front with a large emerald stud which flashed in the light of the candles.

It was such a beautiful stone that Brucena could not keep her eyes from turning towards it, and as if he realised at what she was looking, Lord Rawthorne said:

"I think, Miss Nairn, you are admiring my latest acquisition since I reached India. I wanted to buy it from the Maharajah of Gwalior, but he insisted on making me a present of it. I have been searching ever since to find something to give him in return."

William Sleeman stiffened as his guest spoke. Then he said slowly, as if he was choosing his words:

"I think, My Lord, you would be wise to be careful of accepting gifts from the young Maharajah."

"What do you mean by that?" Lord Rawthorne enquired.

"Only that he has been rather tiresome since he became old enough to take certain things into his own hands. When I spoke to the Governor-General about him a short while ago, he made it clear that we should be particularly careful of 'Greeks when they come bearing gifts.'"

Captain Sleeman spoke in a way which made it impossible to take offence at his words.

But there was a little frown between Lord Rawthorne's eyes as he said:

"I understand quite well what you are saying to me, Sleeman. At the same time, the British Resident says there has been a great deal of unfair gossip about the Maharajah, and he suggested that the British have in many ways treated him unjustly."

Brucena knew it was with effort that Cousin William bit back the words that came to his lips.

There was a great deal that he could say about the behaviour of the young Maharajah, but he knew that it would doubtless be repeated to the Resident and would only make trouble.

The old Maharajah had died six years ago, leaving his widow Baza Bae but no legitimate heir.

After much consultation, she adopted as an heir a relative of her late husband's.

This boy was given the title of Maharajah and grew up at the Court, but soon he showed himself to be a morose, ill-conditioned young devil.

The Gwalior Army had always been turbulent, rebellious, addicted to plunder, and menaced the State and the safety of its neighbours.

The Prince encouraged all the wildest malcontents, and, strangely enough, the British Resident seemed content to let the young Prince do what he liked.

It was the Maharajah and the worst of his soldiers who encouraged the Thugs, and the British
Resident took the attitude that Captain Sleeman's
reports of their activities were exaggerated.

He said to all who would listen that he was
quite certain that many of the hangings and the
imprisonments imposed on the men who were caught
were a miscarriage of justice.

What is more, he refused to allow William Sleeman to pursue or capture any Thug on Gwalior territory.

It was a very difficult situation for Captain Sleeman, and although he had the full authority of the
Governor-General to put down Thuggee and repress
it in every way he could, the proximity of Gwalior
made his task more arduous. He had said so often:
"The Province is a sanctuary for the men I pursue."

Now that she had heard the origin of the
emerald in Lord Rawthorne's shirt-front, it struck
Brucena that it was no longer attractive and had an
almost evil glint in it.

Because the subject had been dropped, William
Sleeman turned to speak to Iain Huntley on some
other matter, and in a voice that only Brucena was
meant to hear, Lord Rawthorne said:

"Emeralds would become you, Miss Nairn. I
would like to see them against your white skin."

She considered his remark to be impertinent and
raised her chin a little as she replied in a cold
voice:

"What other parts of India are you visiting, Lord
Rawthorne?"

He realised why she had changed the subject,
and replied with an annoying twinkle in his eye:

"I am a wanderer without direction or much
purpose, Miss Nairn, and I intend to stay and enjoy
myself wherever my mood takes me."

Brucena did not reply, and Amelie said:

"You must see the Taj Mahal, Lord Rawthorne.

It is one of the most beautiful buildings I have ever seen in my life, and my husband feels the same. My father always said it was one of the great wonders of the world."

"You must forgive me," Lord Rawthorne said, "if I ask the name of your father. I find it rather surprising to find a Frenchwoman here in the centre of India."

"My father belonged to the ancient family of the *Comtes* Blondin de Chalain," Amelie replied, "and he, *Comte* Auguste Blondin de Chalain, who settled in Ile de France, what you call Mauritius, sent me to India because he thought there might be opportunities here to improve his fortune."

Brucena realised that Lord Rawthorne was not only interested in what Amelie was telling him but also impressed that she came from a noble French family.

She despised him because his attitude became a little more respectful as Amelie went on to say that she had only been nineteen when she came to India in 1828 to stay with an English family in Jubbulpore.

It was there that she had met William Sleeman, and, much to the annoyance of a large number of young, very eligible Army officers in the district, had fallen head-over-heels in love with the forty-year-old political officer and married him.

It was certainly not surprising that he had fallen in love with her, for Amelie de Chalain was tall and had very fair skin and dark brown hair. She had a natural vivacity, a quick intelligence, and a charm which had almost every man she met at her feet.

At the moment, however, she was not looking her best, and it was obvious as the evening progressed that Lord Rawthorne had eyes only for Brucena.

He sat himself down beside her when the gentlemen joined the ladies and paid her compliments which did not make her blush but which she disregarded as somewhat impertinent.

She had the feeling that he expected her to be bowled over by his attentions, and the fact that she found him so unattractive made her astonished when she heard William Sleeman say to his wife:

"I have had a letter, my dear, from Mr. Cavendish which makes it imperative that I should see him sooner or later, and Lord Rawthorne has put forward an idea to which I hope you will agree."

"What is that?" Amelie asked.

"His Lordship is very anxious that we should all attend some sports which have been arranged for his amusement while he is in Gwalior. I thought it might amuse you, and of course Brucena, if we all journeyed to Gwalior and stayed with His Lordship in the guest-house which he tells me has been put at his disposal."

Mrs. Sleeman was obviously astonished at her husband's suggestion, knowing what he thought of Gwalior and in particular of the behaviour of the British Resident.

But she was quick-witted enough to realise that he must have an ulterior motive in agreeing to Lord Rawthorne's invitation and with only the faintest pause she replied with a smile:

"It sounds delightful, and I am sure it will be nice for Brucena, who has had rather a dull time since she came to stay with us."

"We must certainly change that," Lord Rawthorne said somewhat heavily. "I will speak to the Maharajah, who seems a most accommodating young man, and arrange for you to see native dancing and all sorts of other things in which I have already found the Court of Gwalior excels."

Because she knew it was expected of her, Brucena said:

"It certainly sounds very interesting."

"It will be, I promise you."

Again in a voice which he intended only for her ears, Lord Rawthorne added:

"I shall do everything personally to make the entertainment especially delightful for you."

She was not surprised that when it was time to say good-bye Lord Rawthorne held her hand far longer than was necessary and looked into her eyes in a manner which she found particularly embarrassing because she was sure Major Huntley had noticed it.

Only when Lord Rawthorne had gone to his own room, escorted by Major Huntley, and Brucena was alone with her cousins did she ask in a voice that was almost a whisper:

"Why do you want to go to Gwalior, Cousin William? I thought you disapproved of the Maharajah."

"You took my breath away," Amelie said, before her husband could reply. "For a moment I thought you must be joking."

"It is an opportunity I have wanted for some time," Captain Sleeman replied. "Always before, when I have entered Gwalior, it has been officially, in my position as Superintendent for the Suppression of Thuggee. If I go there as the guest of a noble Lord, I may deceive a number of people into being off their guard."

"That is what I thought your reason must be," his wife said. "But, William, is it safe? Supposing . . ."

"If it is going to worry you," William Sleeman said quickly, "then we will stay at home."

"No, of course not," Amelie said. "I am not as foolish as that. It is just that we have heard such terrible reports of the Maharajah's behaviour, young though he is, and I believe the way he treats his benefactor, Baza Bae, defies description."

"How can he be so ungrateful after she chose him?" Brucena asked.

"He is a horrible young man. One of my friends

was telling me only the other day how abominably rude he is to the poor woman, and that in fact she is frightened because her very life depends on his whim."

William Sleeman's lips tightened and Brucena knew he was thinking that the British Resident should take a firm hand in the matter, but as there was no point in saying so, they said good-night and went to their rooms.

* * *

Brucena was up early. She always was.

Almost irresistibly, because she hoped against hope that she had been mistaken about the little boy who had haunted her dreams all night, she walked to the end of the garden where she had seen him the morning before.

She looked over the low hibiscus hedge, wondering if the travellers who had been camped there twenty-four hours earlier would be there again.

But the place was empty and there were only the marks left on the sandy ground where the children had played.

She turned away, sick at heart, feeling that even if she told Cousin William of her fears about the child, it would be too late now to save him.

The party of Thugs, if that was what they were, had disappeared and might be anywhere in the Province, or perhaps were on their way to Gwalior, where they would be safe.

"I should have spoken at once," she told herself.

But it had been difficult if not impossible when they had arrived home, because of Lord Rawthorne's presence, and then darkness had fallen and it would have been impossible to find any particular party of travellers when there must have been so many leaving the town after the market closed.

She was just about to walk back to the bungalow

when she saw a tall figure coming through the flower-filled garden and knew it was Lord Rawthorne.

"A servant told me I would find you here," he said. "I was hoping I could persuade you to ride with me this morning."

"I thought you were leaving early," Brucena replied.

"I am in no hurry to do so now that I have met you."

Brucena turned her head aside and he exclaimed:

"You are beautiful! I suppose many men have told you that. I find you the most beautiful thing I have seen since I left England."

"You cannot have looked closely at India or its people," Brucena replied. "I find it, although I have seen very little of it as yet...the most beautiful place I have ever seen, and the Indian women are like dream-Princesses."

"That is exactly what you are," Lord Rawthorne answered in a low voice, "a dream-Princess that I have seen only in my dreams. But now you are real and I have found you."

"You should not be speaking to me like this," Brucena said, starting back along the path towards the bungalow.

"Who will prevent me?" he enquired. "You will learn, as you get to know me better, that I always say what I think."

"Perhaps some thoughts are best kept to one's self," Brucena replied.

He laughed.

"Nonsense! All women like compliments, and what I am saying is only the truth and therefore I am quite certain it is very much more acceptable."

He was so conceited, Brucena thought, that she wished she was clever and witty enough to make him look foolish.

But she could not find the right words and could only walk more swiftly, aware that because he was so tall he towered above her, and feeling inadequate to cope with a man who wasted no time on the preliminaries of courtship, if that was what this was.

As if he knew what she was thinking, Lord Rawthorne stopped suddenly and put out his hand to take her by the wrist and prevent her from going any farther.

"Look at me!" he commanded.

Because she was so surprised at his behaviour, she did what he asked.

"I have thought about you all night." he said. "I think you have bewitched me! I find you entrancing and irresistible!"

He spoke with surprising violence, and Brucena would have moved away if he had not been holding on to her wrist.

"I am afraid, Lord Rawthorne," she said in what she hoped was an icy voice, "I am Scottish enough not to rush impetuously into friendships, but prefer to take my time to get to know people."

"You know it is not friendship I am offering you," Lord Rawthorne replied, "but if it pleases you, I will play your game for a little while. There is something about you which goes to a man's head, and, combined with this climate, I find it very intoxicating."

"Kindly allow me to go back to the house," Brucena said.

She struggled to release her wrist but he held her, and she had the frightened feeling that he was about to put his other arm round her, when to her relief she saw someone coming towards them, and only as she was freed was she aware that it was Major Huntley.

She turned to face him, and he said in a voice which she thought uncomfortably had a note of rebuke in it:

"Your cousin is looking for you, Miss Nairn. You will find him in the Breakfast-Room."

"Thank you, Major Huntley," Brucena replied.

As she spoke she looked at him and saw an expression in his eyes that made her angry.

He was obviously condemning and despising her, and she told herself that he had absolutely no right to look at her in such a way, nor to think that she was in any way to blame for the position in which he had found her.

Because she was so angry she ran away from the two men and hurried towards the house, hoping that they would think it was because she did not wish to keep her cousin waiting but knowing that she was really running from an awkward situation.

It did not in any way assuage her feelings when she discovered that Cousin William was in fact not in the Breakfast-Room and had not sent for her.

Lord Rawthorne stayed the whole of that day, and although Brucena was obliged to speak to him at meals, she managed to keep out of his way at other times.

She knew she had no wish to come into contact with him again, and she said to Amelie:

"I suppose we must go to Gwalior? I am quite happy here, and I feel, from all I have heard, that it will be a horrid place."

"You will enjoy it," Amelie replied, "and William's troubles and difficulties need not worry you. If His Lordship is to be believed, there will be sports and native dancing. You will enjoy every moment of it."

"I suppose so," Brucena said reluctantly.

"But you will!" Amelie insisted. "The first Festival that I attended when I was at Jubbulpore was the most exciting experience I had ever imagined. It was so beautiful, and everyone wore fantastic jewels, even the elephants!"

She laughed as she added:

"My two little rows of pearls seemed very insignificant when compared with the Maharajah's, who has ropes and ropes of them, and of course necklaces of every other precious stone."

"I have read stories about the Indian jewels," Brucena said, "but some of them are unlucky, and that is what I felt last night about Lord Rawthorne's emerald."

As she spoke she wondered if that was the truth. Perhaps it was really because she disliked him that she had felt that the emerald he was wearing was evil.

Then she told herself that jewels did possess strange powers, and she was quite certain that she would never wish to own the emerald which Lord Rawthorne was wearing or any other jewels that had ever belonged to the evil Maharajah.

"Whatever our feelings may be when we are in Gwalior, even if we are shocked by what we see, or affronted by what we hear, we must hide them under a veneer of politeness," Amelie said.

She smiled as she added:

"The only thing I want to do is to help William. You can have no idea how he has dedicated himself body and soul to this crusade of repressing Thuggee, and so far he has been so successful that everyone is amazed at his achievements."

"I am sure they are," Brucena said, "and I am certain he will end up being Knighted for having killed the dragon, and you will be 'My Lady' and have a fine tiara to wear when you return to England."

Amelie laughed and Brucena felt that deep in her shrewd and sensible little French heart was the ambition that one day her husband would be suitably rewarded for his endeavours and the resolve to help in every possible way towards his goal.

It was with relief that Brucena learnt that Lord Rawthorne intended to leave early in the afternoon so as to start his long journey back to Gwalior.

"There is no hurry," he had said when William Sleeman suggested he should leave before luncheon. "I can travel very swiftly on horse-back, which is why I refused the offer of a carriage from my tour."

"Even with horses you should not wish to travel after dark," Captain Sleeman warned.

Lord Rawthorne laughed somewhat derisively.

"Still worrying about the Thugs, Captain? It is unlikely they will slip a yellow scarf round my throat."

"It is always wise to be fore-armed," William Sleeman said quietly.

"I have been," Lord Rawthorne laughed, "and if I listened to you I should suspect every shadow behind every tree and imagine there is a Thug waiting to get me! Personally, I only see those sort of things after a very thick night."

He laughed again uproariously, and Brucena wished she could throw something at him.

But William Sleeman was apparently quite unperturbed.

"We will look forward to joining Your Lordship in three weeks' time."

"I have changed my mind," Lord Rawthorne said. "I cannot wait so long. I will get back tonight and shall spend tomorrow making all the preparations for your entertainment that have not been made already, and I shall expect you in eight days. I shall be counting every hour eagerly until you appear."

He was speaking to William Sleeman, but he was looking at Brucena and she was angry because she felt herself begin to blush.

He was making his feelings for her far too obvious, and while Cousin William apparently did not notice it, she was sure that Major Huntley did.

Because she felt angry, she walked out through

the open window onto the verandah and moved along
it a little way to stand looking at the flowers in
the garden.

It was very hot but she found surprisingly
that she liked the heat and did not find it oppressive
as a great number of other English people did.

She knew, because it was getting so late in the
year, that it was now possible to move about even
at midday and in the early afternoon, but otherwise
the British usually rose very early and slept after
luncheon as all the Indians did.

From where she stood she could see what appeared to be rolled-up bundles in the shelter of the
shrubs and at the foot of the trees, but it was in fact
the gardeners having their siesta.

This would last for at least two hours, and she
knew that the rest of the servants in other parts of
the bungalow were doing the same.

She heard footsteps and turned to find Lord
Rawthorne advancing towards her.

"I came to say good-bye," he said, "but it is in
fact *au revoir*."

"Good-bye, My Lord."

"You know how much I want to see you again,"
Lord Rawthorne said, covering her hand with both
of his. "I have a great deal to say to you and a great
deal I want you to say to me. It will be easier in
Gwalior—I will see to that!"

Brucena hoped he would do nothing of the
sort, but she could not say so.

He looked at her for a long moment, and then
before she could prevent it he raised her hand to
his lips.

She felt his mouth on her skin and knew that
for some reason which she could not explain to herself, it made her shiver.

Then with relief she heard her cousin come out
onto the verandah and she was free.

As Lord Rawthorne rode off, with the soldiers

of the Gwalior Cavalry behind him, she felt an inexpressible relief that he had gone.

"Can His Lordship really like the Maharajah and what he has found in Gwalior?" she heard Major Huntley ask.

"He has reasons for his preferences," William Sleeman answered, "and as far as I am concerned, he has given me an opportunity I have waited for for some time, and I am not prepared to quarrel with him."

"No, of course not," Iain Huntley agreed. "At the same time, I find him insupportable."

'So do I,' Brucena wanted to say.

Then she remembered the suspicion she had seen in Major Huntley's eyes, and felt angrily that she would not stoop to explain herself.

'Let him think what he likes,' she thought. 'He is in his own way almost as unpleasant as Lord Rawthorne.'

She started to walk along the verandah towards the open window.

"Where are you going?" William Sleeman asked.

"To pack my prettiest gowns to dazzle Gwalior," Brucena answered, "and of course the charming Lord Rawthorne!"

She was speaking sarcastically, but it pleased her to see the sudden anger flash in Major Huntley's eyes and to notice the definite scowl on his face.

Did he really think she was infatuated with that conceited popinjay? she asked herself. And if he did, how could he be so stupid?

There really was quite a lot of packing to do, and the maid-servants in the bungalow were kept busy pressing Amelie's and Brucena's gowns.

Not for one moment had Brucena regretted the money from her precious store which she had expended on new gowns.

She had read enough about India before she had left England to realise that because of the heat one had to change frequently, and she was glad that she had enough gowns at least for the next few months.

Nevertheless, she was very touched and extremely grateful when Amelie gave her some of her own clothes that she could no longer wear.

"You will want them again," Brucena protested. "I cannot take them."

Amelie smiled.

"I will let you in on a secret," she said. "My father spoils me, and through me he has made a great deal of money, while William has received a great deal of credit."

Brucena looked curious and she explained:

"The reason I came to India was that my father wanted me to spy out the land for him and report to him what I thought of the sugar-cane which a certain Captain William Sleeman had imported from Tahiti."

She gave a little laugh.

"Poor William did not know then that the best sugar-canes come from Mauritius."

She smiled as she went on:

"I had quite a job convincing him that our canes were far superior to his, but he asked me to get him some and my father sent him the seeds."

She saw Brucena's interest and went on:

"I do not have to tell you the end of the story! The Mauritius sugar-cane flourished, William was complimented by the Government for all he has done for agriculture, and Papa made a great deal of money in the process!"

Brucena clapped her hands together.

"What a lovely story, and all the more exciting because it is true."

"It was not only the sugar-cane that interested him," Amelie said with a soft note in her voice. "From the moment I saw him with his blue eyes and his clever forehead, I knew he was the man I had been looking for all my life."

"Did you really fall in love the moment you saw him?" Brucena asked.

"Not at the first moment," Amelie admitted truthfully, "but after we had talked together and I realised how different he was from all the young men who paid me compliments and only wanted to dance, I knew he was the only man I had ever wanted to marry."

"He was very much older than you," Brucena said.

"Yes," Amelie agreed. "I was nineteen while he was forty and a confirmed bachelor! But love has nothing to do with age. Love is irresistible, and when you find it, my dear, you will understand what I mean."

Brucena gave a little sigh.

"I hope so," she said, "but sometimes I feel I shall never fall in love."

Amelie gave a wise little laugh.

"You will," she said. "Suddenly your heart turns upside-down, the air is full of music, and indeed, once you have found the man who previously was only part of your dreams, the world is never the same again."

"I hope I will be as lucky as you," Brucena said.

She did not sound very optimistic.

She had the feeling as she spoke that her heart was rather different from Cousin Amelie's, much more practical and down-to-earth, and where the French would find romance wherever they looked, she was made of sterner stuff.

'I wish I were not,' she thought. 'I want to fall in love. I want to be married and happy as Amelie is with Cousin William.'

Then she thought of Lord Rawthorne, and she shivered.

If that was the type of man who was going to

ask her to marry him, then she would rather remain an old maid all her life!

She told herself that when she reached Gwalior she would have to be careful ... very careful not to be alone with him, and the one thing she wanted to avoid above all else was for him to touch her again.

She had washed her hand a number of times since he had kissed it, and yet very annoyingly she could still feel his lips, hot, possessive, and demanding, on her skin.

When she went to bed that night Brucena looked out into the darkness.

The stars were brilliant overhead and there was the fragrance of the flowers and the scent of woodsmoke.

It was a night made for romance, the whisperings of lovers, the songs sung passionately beside the shimmering water of the lake, a note passed from hand to hand, from lips to lips.

Yet Brucena was not thinking of love, but of the little boy, a child with a tear-streaked face holding tightly in his hand a ball of pure silk.

Where was he now? Where had he been taken?

Was he being initiated into the terrible cult of the goddess of darkness—Kali?

She suddenly felt as if the horror and terror of the murderers were encroaching on her and she could not escape from them.

It was one thing to read about the Thugs, even to think about them, but another to feel that they were moving out there in the darkness, intent on enjoying their lust to kill as an Englishman might enjoy the pleasure of big-game hunting.

The only difference was that they were dedicated, their whole life given to their foul, murderous religion.

It suddenly seemed to Brucena as if the very anonymity of it was so horrifying because one had no idea where to look for a Thug and no means of identifying him.

They were in the darkness, waiting, their thirst for blood yearning to be appeased, their whole purpose to kill and go on killing secretly and in most cases without fear of identification or capture.

"How can one man like Cousin William, who had first revealed the whole horror of Thuggee and now continued to fight it almost single-handed, ever win?" she asked herself.

Whatever the rights or wrongs, he was pitting his strength single-handed against something which had existed for centuries and which was deeply ingrained in generations of Thugs.

"It is useless! It is a hopeless cause!" Brucena cried in her mind.

Then she saw again the little boy's face with the tears running down his cheeks, and Cousin William with his steady blue eyes lit with the zeal of a visionary swearing he would stamp out "this abomination" now and forever!

Chapter Four

William Sleeman was determined that his wife should travel slowly and that the journey to Gwalior should be a pleasant one.

Ordinarily he would have taken the journey himself without undue hurry in five days, but with Amelie and Brucena with him, he was determined that they should enjoy the countryside and he would also take the opportunity of inspecting various of his own territories on the way.

He was amused by Lord Rawthorne's insistence that they arrive as soon as possible, and he was not so obtuse as not to realise that the reason was a desire to see Brucena rather than to entertain them with the festivities he was arranging in their honour.

However, he considered his own interests more important.

He therefore sent a number of messengers ahead to arrange for him to see the officials in the territories through which he would be passing and also instructed them to make sure that the accommodation in which they stayed was the best available.

Brucena was impressed by the precise and methodical way in which Cousin William had planned the journey.

They set out very early three days later, travelling in what she appreciated was a particularly smart

69

turn-out with four fine bays pulling their carriage, which she knew had cost a large amount of money.

They were escorted as usual by Sepoys and Cavalrymen and when she exclaimed at how Royal the entourage looked, Cousin William had laughed.

"If we had not had to get there so quickly," he had said, "we should have done it in real style, as I intend to travel next year when I carry out inspections."

"Will you look more important than you do at the moment?" Brucena had asked.

"Certainly," he had said, "because then I shall be preceded by an elephant and carried in a palanquin."

He smiled as if he mocked himself as he had added:

"In my befeathered, cocked hat I really inspire respect and admiration even from the Thugs!"

Brucena regretted the absence of the elephant, but she enjoyed the excitement their horses and carriage caused wherever they appeared.

She soon learnt that Cousin William was not only respected but trusted—one might even say loved—by the people in his Province.

Many of them already realised the relief they enjoyed from the oppressive menace of the Thugs. They could travel more safely and were not blackmailed into silence as undoubtedly they had been in the past.

When Brucena said this to Cousin William when they were alone, he shook his head.

"There is still a great deal more to be done," he said, "and I am not really happy in knowing that if I drive them out of this Province they will merely menace the people in other parts of India."

She knew as they journeyed on that he was thinking all the time of how difficult Gwalior was making his work by allowing the Thugs to take refuge there.

He had already, although she was not aware of it, confided to Iain Huntley that it would be of tremendous help if the visit gave them an inkling as to which of the wanted men were seen in Gwalior.

"Do you really think they will show themselves?" Major Huntley asked.

"Remember, a lot of them have no idea that we are even aware of their existence. But you and I have our secret list of names. I am certain that a great number of those on it think themselves anonymous."

"That is true," Iain Huntley agreed, "and we must certainly keep our eyes open."

"I am relying on you mostly to do that," William Sleeman replied, "and you know how successful you have been in the past when I have sent you on missions which I thought no-one else could bring to a satisfactory conclusion."

"Thank you."

The two men smiled at each other and they both knew that in this struggle they were grateful for each other's comradeship and understanding.

There was in fact no-one else in whom William Sleeman could confide.

He had no wish to spoil the romantic happiness that he had with Amelie by harrowing her with the unsavoury details of his work.

Of course, she knew a certain amount about it, but he tried when he was at home to interest her in other things, and they had a close bond in common in the subject of agriculture and sugar-canes, through which they had first met.

William Sleeman was also extremely interested in trees.

When the Government had congratulated him on the huge success of the Mauritius sugar-canes, to celebrate the occasion he had started to plant an impressive avenue of trees from Jhansi Ghat, on the Nerbudda River, to Mirzapur on the Ganges.

The fruit that the trees were to bear was to be left every year for travellers to enjoy, and he somewhat ironically had the trees planted and nurtured by former Thugs under his direction.

This had made him study the flora of India more closely than he had done before, and Amelie with his help made some delightful sketches of flowers and plants that they knew would interest their friends at home in England.

While they drove North towards Gwalior, Cousin William pointed out to Brucena everything he thought she would find interesting, and she found that he usually had fascinating stories to tell about the people they passed on the road.

She learnt things from him such as that nine Hindus out of ten throughout India believed the rainbow to derive from the breath of a snake, and that a shooting-star meant that a great man had been born that night, or a great man had died.

Then one day on the journey when Amelie fell asleep, he told Brucena some of the superstitions that she had longed to know about the Thugs.

In a voice so low that his wife could not overhear, William Sleeman said that before setting out on their expeditions to murder, the Thugs make their obligations to Kali and to Bhowani, the goddess of smallpox.

Before they left, some of the gang would proceed in the direction they were about to take to observe the flight of the birds and to listen to the chirping of the lizards.

"What is the meaning of those sounds?" Brucena asked.

"The lizard chirping," William Sleeman replied, "or a crow making a noise on a living tree on the left side are good."

"And are there others?" Brucena enquired.

"A great number," he answered. "The appearance of a tiger is deemed an excellent sign, and the noise of a partridge on the right side of the road denotes that they will meet with good booty on that very spot. Accordingly, they will wait there for their unfortunate victim."

"And what signs forecast bad luck?" Brucena questioned.

"A hare or a snake crossing the road before them, an owl screeching, and the noise of a single jackal."

"It all sounds very complicated."

"I am glad to say it does make their task more difficult," her cousin replied. "It is unlucky to murder a person of the Kamale caste, and also metal-workers, carpenters, washer-men, stone-cutters, pot-makers, and lepers!"

Brucena gave a little cry.

"That does not seem to leave many potential victims."

"They find enough," William Sleeman said drily, "and many a party of travellers owe their lives because amongst them there was a man driving a cow or a female goat."

"Do Thugs strangle only the rich?" Brucena enquired.

William Sleeman shook his head.

"There is no difference for them between rich and poor, for theirs is a religious duty."

"I cannot think why you chose the very difficult task of suppressing these particular people."

"I think God did that for me," William Sleeman said simply, and Brucena knew he believed that that was the truth.

Amelie awoke and they went back to the subject of trees and flowers.

Many of the people they passed on the first part of their journey were walking and had a pack-horse or a donkey on which to carry their goods.

Two days later they saw the Lohars in their handsome wooden bullock-carts that were studded with brass inlays and nails, with wheels carved with the signs of the Zodiac.

Brucena exclaimed about them and William Sleeman explained:

"The carts creep from village to village as the Lohars apply their hereditary trade of making fine tools."

"Do they travel all over India?"

"They wander because in the sixteenth century," William Sleeman replied, "when their Rajah Pratap Singh was defeated by the Moslems, the tribe made a vow that its people would never live in Rajasthan until Pratap Singh was King again. They are still hoping that someday he will return."

It was this sort of story that made the journey pass quickly for Brucena, and she slept peacefully at night to dream of the mango groves, the banyan trees, and the little villages where the elders clustered in the shade while the children played naked with one another on the dusty brown earth.

The mud huts, the bullocks dragging clumsy wooden ploughs, the sudden sight of a clump of hibiscus flowers, the smell of wood-smoke and blossom, and occasionally the music of a flute, had a magic that Brucena felt she could never describe to anyone who had not actually seen it.

They sometimes stopped for quite a long time while William Sleeman consulted with the elders of a village or received a report from one of the District Officers.

There, young men always looked at Brucena with admiration when they met and wistfully when they departed, leaving the Englishman to a lonely existence in which he coped with the problems and difficulties which arose daily and unceasingly in small Indian communities over an area of hundreds of square miles.

At last, when it seemed that they had travelled for an interminable time, they moved into the undulating country of Gwalior, which was very different in every way from the land through which they had just passed.

There were rivers and many more trees than they had seen previously, and finally in the distance a great red Fort topped a precipitous ridge, appearing to menace the town beneath it.

The Fort had a long and lurid history. Rajput women had destroyed themselves by fire between its walls. The Moghuls had poisoned prisoners by giving them the juice of poppies mixed with poisonous flowers.

Several times the British had captured the Fort and returned it to Sindhia.

"I cannot help feeling," William Sleeman said, as he looked ahead, "that we are approaching the Capital of a Dynasty of barbarian Princes who, like Attila, would choose their place of residence as the devils choose Pandemonium."

"Be careful what you say, dearest," Amelie begged him.

"I have hated Gwalior," he replied, "ever since the first time I came here. Before I reached my camp, a gang of thieves had stolen one of my best carpets and the brass brackets of my tent-poles!"

The way he spoke made both Amelie and Brucena laugh.

"Let me warn you to be careful," he said seriously. "I remember a minor Rajah who came here some years ago to pay his respects to the then Maharajah of Gwalior—he had all his jewels, clothes, and valuables rifled."

Amelie put her hand up to her neck as she said:

"I wish I had not brought my pearls with me."

"That same Rajah," her husband went on, "also lost five horses, and he warned me that I should cut off the tails of all my horses or they would certainly be panicked from the camp and ridden off into the night."

"Are things just as bad now?" Amelie asked.

"I would not be surprised," William Sleeman said, "although I imagine that as we are guests of Lord Rawthorne, we will be fairly safe. Yet thieves are thieves wherever you may find them. I advise you both to keep with you always anything you have of value."

"I cannot understand why you did not tell me about this earlier," Amelie complained.

William Sleeman laughed.

"I was rather afraid that if I did, you might refuse to come at the last moment. As I wished to get into Gwalior without offending the Resident by saying I am here on business, I thought it best to keep silent."

"It was very naughty of you, dearest," Amelie said.

But both William Sleeman and Brucena knew she was not really angry.

Their reception was certainly impressive. Guns were fired, Lord Rawthorne rode out to meet them with a detachment of Cavalry carrying penants, flowers were thrown into their carriage, and great crowds of people cheered as they drove through the town towards the Palace.

The old town of Gwalior was a mile and a half from the new town of Lashkar—the Camp, so named when the previous Maharajah, a war-like man, had pitched his tents there in 1809.

He had started to erect a permanent building surrounded by a Park or Compound so vast that, Brucena was told later, tigers strolled through it thinking they were still in their own wild territory!

The Palace was very impressive as it was surrounded with crimson bougainvillaea.

There was the din of a vast number of kettledrums and the braying of barbaric trumpets; then, passing the Palace itself, they came to a smaller building which Lord Rawthorne, now riding beside them, told them was his guest-house.

They stepped out and Brucena thought that despite the annoying manner in which Lord Rawthorne was looking at her, despite all that Cousin William had said about Gwalior, she was glad that she had come.

Lord Rawthorne was in his element and had obviously been given *carte blanche* by the Maharajah to entertain his guests as he wished. There appeared to be an army of servants to look after them, and Brucena and Amelie's rooms were decorated with a profusion of flowers.

"He is certainly being very attentive," Amelie said as she and Brucena went to their bedrooms to freshen themselves up after their journey. "I am quite certain if William and I had come without you, our welcome would not have been so overwhelming."

Brucena laughed.

"At least I have my uses!"

Amelie looked at her reflectively.

"His Lordship is very presentable and, I believe, very rich."

"If you are match-making," Brucena replied, "you can forget it. If you want the truth, I find him rather repulsive."

"An English Lord has great importance, I believe," Amelie said.

"That is true," Brucena agreed, "but, being English, I have no wish for an arranged marriage. So stop scheming, Amelie! When I do decide to become someone's wife, I want to be in love."

"I can still go on scheming!" Amelie flashed. "You would look very pretty in a coronet."

"And so would you," Brucena retorted, "but instead of looking for a French *Duc* or at least a *Comte*, like your father, you settled for an English political officer who lives in the wilds of Saugor!"

"That is true!" Amelie exclaimed. "But William is different, and far more attractive than any other man in the world. So you can give up looking for his equal!"

"Whatever you may say, I shall still go on hoping to find another William!" Brucena retorted, and went to her own bedroom.

There were two Indian maids to wait on her and as she took off her bonnet she saw a note on her dressing-table.

She guessed who it was from and did not open it until she had changed her gown.

Then somewhat reluctantly she took it up in her fingers, feeling that Lord Rawthorne was already encroaching on her in a manner which she was sure he would maintain for the whole of her stay.

She had found herself understanding Amelie's assertion that he was in fact a very eligible *parti* and that any other girl in her position would encourage his advances and hope fervently that he would propose marriage.

Brucena could not explain her feelings about him. She only knew they were there, and that she not only found him unpleasant but actively disliked him.

She had been sure of it when she had seen his eyes searching her face on arrival and had known when he took her hand as they entered the guest-house that the mere proximity of him made her flesh creep.

"It is absurd, and I am quite certain I should not allow it to happen," she told herself. "But it does, and I only hope he does not manoeuvre me into a position where I am alone with him."

She was quite certain that that was what he intended to do, and she opened the letter wondering what he would say.

His writing was what she expected, she thought, bold and large, and the note was written in a manner which was almost as if he ordered her to appreciate what he said.

Welcome, my Dream Princess. I have been counting the hours until your arrival, and now I kiss your hand in greeting and hope for very much more.

Brucena dropped the letter down on the dressing-table and turned away from the mirror.

"Thank you very much," she said in Urdu to her two attendants, and they giggled with delight because she had spoken their language.

They bowed and put their hands together, palm to palm, as they left the room.

The Sitting-Room, which was in the centre of the building, was decorated with a huge chandelier which, Brucena was to find later, was very characteristic of the decoration of the main Palace.

The previous Maharajah had liked everything to glitter, so that not only the chandelier but even the furniture glinted with pieces of crystal, polished gold, and engraved glass.

There were cool drinks in the Sitting-Room and little sweetmeats that were delicious but, as Amelie said regretfully, extremely fattening.

There was also Lord Rawthorne, who seemed larger and more overpowering than he had in Saugor.

"I have planned very exciting things for you tomorrow," he said, "but I thought tonight you would like to be quiet after your journey. So we will just dine here *en famille,* although of course His Highness is longing to meet you."

"It sounds delightful," Amelie said politely.

"I have been enjoying the tiger-shooting," Lord Rawthorne continued. "I do not know, Sleeman, whether you or Huntley wish to take part in a shoot while you are here. I can certainly arrange one which will guarantee you several fine animals at the end of the day."

Lord Rawthorne continued to describe how well he had shot and how many animals he had already bagged, but Brucena had ceased to listen to him.

She was looking out into the flower-filled garden and the Compound in which the Palace with its guest-houses stood, and was wondering if it would ever be possible for her to go into the town and see the people.

Perhaps, if luck was on her side, she would have a glimpse of the little boy she had never forgotten.

However, she had an idea that they would be cut off from having any contact with the ordinary people, and while she was still wondering, the door opened and the Honourable Richard Cavendish, Resident of Gwalior, was announced.

There was no doubt that he was extremely annoyed that Captain Sleeman, whom he had forbidden to capture or harass any Thugs in the Province of Gwalior, was actually here in person.

But he had the good sense not to say anything provocative, though it was obvious from the expression on his face and the tone of his voice that they could expect no welcome from him.

"That I am surprised to see you, Sleeman," he said, "is to express my feelings very mildly!"

"I found it impossible to refuse Lord Rawthorne's most generous invitation," William Sleeman replied blithely, "besides which, my wife and I were most eager to show a little of India to my cousin who was recently arrived from England to stay with us. Let me introduce you."

Mr. Cavendish greeted Brucena with what she thought was bad grace, but because she thought it would please her cousin, she asked questions about Gwalior to which he was bound to reply.

Fortunately, Lord Rawthorne had invited the Resident to dinner, and when the ladies retired to rest before dinner, Amelie said:

"It was almost worth coming all this way to see how much it annoys Mr. Cavandish. He never expected to find William on his territory and in a position where he cannot order him to leave!"

"I think he is a horrid man," Brucena said, "apart from the fact that he allows the Thugs so much licence."

"I agree with you," Amelie replied, "but we must be careful for William's sake to be charming to everyone."

And that, Brucena thought with a sinking of her heart, included Lord Rawthorne.

Dinner was a fairly quiet meal as they all were tired, but after it was over, Lord Rawthorne insisted that they should go out onto the verandah and look at the lights of the town below them, at the great precipice at their back, and at the countryside stretching out towards a far horizon.

With the cliffs and gorges, mango groves and a winding river, it was very beautiful as the sun sank.

There were lights coming out one by one and Brucena knew that she would find it very romantic and exciting if Lord Rawthorne had not taken the opportunity of standing unnecessarily close to her and attempting to speak to her alone.

"I have so much to show you, so much to talk to you about," he said in a voice that he thought only she could hear.

"I am too tired tonight to appreciate anything," she replied.

"You received my note?"

"Yes."

"There were so many other things I wanted to write, but I thought I would rather say them."

"I hope that is something you will not do."

"You will not be able to stop me."

"Then I shall be extremely angry."

"Will it really make you angry to be told that you have haunted me ever since I left Saugor," he asked, "and that only by pretending that you were in my arms have I been able to sleep?"

Brucena moved some steps away from him and he followed her to say:

"Now have I made you angry?"

"Yes, very! You are not to speak to me in such a familiar manner. It is quite outrageous after such a short acquaintance."

"It does not seem short to me. I feel I have known you for years and have been looking for you all my life."

"We actually met only forty-eight hours ago."

"If it were forty-eight minutes or forty-eight years, I should feel exactly the same," Lord Rawthorne said.

His face was very near to hers, and because she had no idea how to cope with the situation, she hurried all the way down the verandah to join Amelie, who was talking to Major Huntley.

"I am tired, Amelie," she said, "and I am sure you are. I think we should go to bed."

"You are quite right, Brucena," Amelie said. "There is always tomorrow in which to see everything. Good-night, Lord Rawthorne, and thank you for your kind and generous welcome."

She curtseyed.

"Good-night, Major Huntley."

Both men bowed as Brucena curtseyed too, but then Lord Rawthorne put out his hand as if to stop her from leaving.

"I want to talk to you," he said. "Must you go?"

"I am sorry," Brucena replied, "but I can barely keep my eyes open."

She hurried quickly after Amelie and they went

together to their bedrooms, which were on the other side of the guest-house.

"Lord Rawthorne is obviously extremely enamoured of you," Amelie said.

"He is far too forward and says things he has no right to say," Brucena remarked.

"Promise me one thing."

"What is that?"

"If he does propose, that you will not turn him down immediately, but will think it over. It would, as you must know, be a brilliant marriage for you, and I assure you that although William and I could produce a number of attractive men who would meet with your approval, they would not be of Lord Rawthorne's social standing, nor would they be likely to possess much money except for what they earn."

"I have told you what I want," Brucena answered.

"I would not ask you to marry for money and position," Amelie said after a moment's pause, "but you might at least try to find love where these things are."

Brucena laughed.

"Now, dearest Amelie, you are being very French!"

She kissed her and went to her own room, where she stood looking out into the night.

"Suppose I never find love?" she asked herself. "But it would be impossible for me to find satisfaction with anything less than what I have hoped for in my dreams."

She knew the future was a very unknown quantity, for she had no wish to return to Scotland to her fault-finding father and jealous Stepmother.

But she would not be able to stay with the Sleemans forever, and she knew that however much she might protest, Amelie would not let her look after her baby as she intended but was already searching for a good Ayah whom other Englishwomen could recommend.

As Brucena had protested, she had said:

"You can certainly help me supervise the baby, and of course I want him with me as much as possible. At the same time, I do not want to bore William, and I know that however pleased he will be with his child, he will still want to have me alone."

"That is when I can look after the baby," Brucena said firmly.

"With the help of an Ayah," Amelie said. "Do not be ridiculous, Brucena. You are far too young and attractive to want to tie yourself to a child. It is men you should be thinking about, and one in particular who will be your future husband."

"Until this paragon of all virtues turns up," Brucena laughed, "I might as well make myself useful."

She was sure that Amelie would let her do nothing of the sort and that once she began to trust the Ayah it would become obvious that she could not impose on their hospitality any more.

The alternative, of course, was to encourage Lord Rawthorne, not that he needed any encouragement.

"It is no use!" Brucena whispered into the night. "I cannot like him, and no amount of persuasion will ever make me feel any differently!"

She could hear mosquitos buzzing in the darkness and she quickly summoned her maids to come and undress her, then crept under the folds of the mosquito-netting. When she lay down she fell asleep almost immediately.

* * *

There was no doubt that Lord Rawthorne had excelled himself in his efforts to entertain Brucena, and there was no pretending that anyone else mattered.

It was her face he watched as the elephants encrusted with silver paint and bearing silver howdahs moved into position, looking in the early-morning mist like great prehistoric monsters, their great forelegs heaving as the howdahs rocked.

Two Squadrons of the Gwalior Lancers jingled past and the excited crowds waited for what Brucena knew would be the great moment of the parade.

There was a smell of damp earth, for the whole ground had been drenched with water from hundreds of goat-skin bags so that the small party sitting on valuable Persian carpets, and under the shade of silk umbrellas, should not be incommoded by the dust.

There was a roll of kettle-drums, the blare of many trumpets, and now through the mist came a huge elephant, far larger than the others, strewn with jewels and carrying on his back a golden howdah in which was seated the young Maharajah.

One look at his ugly, evil face told Brucena that Cousin William was right in everything he had said about him.

He clambered down a ladder from the elephant and they were all presented by Lord Rawthorne. She wondered if the people cheering and turning to him really accepted him as their divinely appointed Ruler.

The Maharajah joined them, seated on a chair that was not unlike a throne and protected from the sun not only by a gold umbrella but by fans made of peacocks' feathers.

Then the entertainment began.

There were marching soldiers, jugglers, magicians, snake-charmers, and acrobats.

"The dancing girls are being kept for tonight," Lord Rawthorne said. "They will doubtless amuse the other men, but I shall have eyes only for you."

"Tell me about the snake-charmers," Brucena said, trying to change the subject from herself.

"You charm me in a manner that I cannot describe," Lord Rawthorne said. "You have caught me in a spell from which I can never escape!"

Try as she would, Brucena could get him to talk of nothing but herself.

By the time the entertainment was over and they were driving back to the Palace, she thought that while what she had watched was fascinating, she wished that Cousin William or even Major Huntley had been able to explain it to her, rather than her having to listen to Lord Rawthorne turning everything she said into an over-effusive compliment.

"I must say," William Sleeman said, when they were alone, "our host makes his feelings very obvious, Brucena. I think perhaps as your Guardian I should ask him if his intentions are strictly honourable!"

He was teasing her, but Brucena rose almost angrily to the bait:

"You are to do nothing of the sort, Cousin William!" she said. "I do my best to discourage His Lordship. If you want the truth, he has completely spoilt the morning for me. I wanted to know the history of what was happening, but he could do nothing but make ridiculous compliments, even including one about my eye-lashes!"

"Well, they are rather long!" William Sleeman said.

Brucena stamped her foot, then realised he was laughing at her, and she began to laugh too.

"Brucena is being quite ridiculous!" Amelie said. "She ought to be delighted that the most eligible man we have ever seen in this part of the world is at her feet, instead of which all she does is to kick him away. You should speak severely to her, William."

"I have a feeling it is due to Brucena's Cornish blood," William Sleeman said. "It makes every one

of us an idealist. I had decided never to marry, until
I met you, my darling, and then look what happened!"

"Oh, William, was I really what you had been
looking for all the years you had remained a bachelor?" Amelie asked, breaking into French as she
always did when she was moved or excited.

"I have told you so often what I felt," her husband said, a little embarrassed because Brucena was
listening, "and I will tell you again, but not at this
moment. We have to get ready for luncheon, at which
we are to meet all the important dignitaries of
Gwalior, and a very unprepossessing lot they are!"

"Be careful, William!" Amelie said quickly. "You
know in this place even the walls have ears!"

It was not until late in the afternoon when it
was growing cooler that Brucena, carrying a sunshade
over her head, slipped out through her bedroom window and into the garden.

She was anxious to avoid letting Lord Rawthorne know where she was going because she was
quite certain he would insist on accompanying her,
and that would spoil everything.

She wanted to wander round by herself. She
wanted to see without having to talk about it, without
everything she said being changed into something
personal.

She kept out of sight of the windows of the
guest-house by moving between the great banks of
bougainvillaea.

The garden was a sheer delight, with the exotic
flowers, and the creepers that climbed over and round
the trees from which the frangipani petals fell like
snow-flakes onto the ground beneath them.

There was no doubt that the surroundings were
beautiful, and it was a pity, Brucena thought, that
the characters of the people who lived in Gwalior
did not match the beauty of the place.

The Compound in which the Palace was situated was so enormous that it held, as is usual in India, a vast number of people living in it, all of whom, she was sure, served the Maharajah in one capacity or another.

There were servants in his special uniform moving from some low houses at the back towards the Palace, and there were soldiers whom she had seen on parade, now off duty, who were camping in tents in another part of the Park.

Then she saw children playing amongst the low houses from which came the smell of cooking, while smoke, white and thick, rose slowly over them with no breeze to blow it away.

Most of them, Brucena saw at a glance, were not as pretty as the children she had seen at Saugor, and in particular one child, of whom she was still thinking, and who, if she was honest, she was trying to find.

There were men, heavily moustachioed and bearded, sitting under banyan trees, deep in conversation.

They made her think of the men she had seen with the little boy who was crying.

These too were wearing turbans, white-sashed dhotis over pantaloons, and sandals with curled toes.

"A description," she told herself, "which might apply to millions of men all over India."

Several men looked up as she passed them, but they did not seem to be particularly interested, and she walked on, moving amongst the trees, passing shrubs and flowers, then finding more low houses crowded with people.

She knew it was nothing unusual, because she had read that most Indian servants, when they were fortunate enough to have a job with the Maharajah or someone in the East India Company, supported perhaps ten or fifteen relatives. Wherever he went, they went too.

There were many lean dogs looking for scraps

and occasionally a tethered goat struggling to find grass on the dried-up, sun-baked ground that badly needed rain.

'I must go back,' Brucena thought; 'it will soon be time to change for dinner.'

Then, turning round the side of a clump of flowering bushes, she came upon half-a-dozen children playing together under some trees.

They were of various ages and she saw as she looked at them that they were all boys, and each one seemed a little more attractive than the last.

She had a feeling, although she could not be sure, that they came from many different castes.

They were playing happily with one another, some with small sticks, others with stones.

Then as she stood watching them, she saw the boy she sought—or rather, to be truthful, he saw her.

He was standing a little detached from the rest, as if he was shy and afraid to join them.

Then his eyes, unusually serious, which seemed to fill his small face, lighted up and he came towards her just as he had done the first morning.

Now he had no flower, but when he reached her he put his hand into the breast of the clothes he wore and drew out what with a leap of her heart she expected—the little ball of pink silk that she had given him!

She crouched down so that her face was level with his.

"You have your pink ball," she said in Urdu. "I was looking for you."

He smiled at her and she thought that although she spoke haltingly, he understood.

"Where is your mother?" she asked.

For a moment he looked puzzled; then as she repeated the question, an expression of pain came into his face and his eyes filled with tears.

"Mother dead," he said, and as he spoke he put his hand up to his neck.

Brucena drew in her breath as she knew she had found out what she wanted to know.

She thought quickly whether there was anything more she could say or could give him, then some instinct warned her that it was dangerous.

But she could not leave him, could not go away when he had recognised her, and she felt in some way that he trusted her.

Because she had nothing else, she took off the white silk tassel that was attached to her sunshade and put it into his hand.

He looked at it with delight.

"For you!" she said.

"Mine?" he questioned, as he had before.

"Yes, yours."

He was obviously delighted, but he did not run and jump as he had done with the children with whom she had first seen him.

Instead he just stood, holding the tassel against him, the pink ball also in his hand.

It was then that Brucena saw a man coming through the trees opposite where the children were playing.

He was tall and moustachioed, and she knew from his turban and his white-sashed dhoti that he was one of the men she had seen with the small boy on the road.

She rose and said deliberately in English:

"Good-bye."

As if the boy was too intent on his new trophy to be interested, she moved away, aware only as she went that the man coming towards her was watching her.

She had the uncomfortable feeling that if she looked at him, she would see an expression of suspicion on his face.

Chapter Five

Brucena thought the entertainment seemed to go on interminably.

At any other time she knew she would have been thrilled and delighted with the dancing of the women, the snake-charmers, and the strange musical instruments whose melody she was beginning to appreciate.

But she found it hard to prevent her thoughts from returning again and again to the little boy who she knew was in the possession of the Thugs.

There was no doubt that the men she had seen him with on the road must have killed the whole party of travellers, but, as she had learnt from her books, they had saved the child because he was attractive.

For what reason, she did not like to question too closely.

The Maharajah who had received them was like a Prince in a fairy-tale and only his face betrayed the fact that he was the villain rather than the hero.

His clothes were embroidered with gold, his *achkan* was sewn with jewels, there were more jewels in his turban, besides a great aigrette pinned to the gold tissue, while ropes of pear-shaped diamonds were looped about it like tinsel on a Christmas-tree.

Jewels flashed on his fingers and blazed on the gold on his sword-belt, while the hilt of his sword was encrusted with diamonds and topped by a single emerald the size of a rupee.

There were ropes and ropes of magnificent pearls round his neck, and Brucena thought wryly that Amelie had been quite right in thinking that her two little strings of pearls would not be noticed.

At the same time, while the Maharajah was obviously prepared to be pleasant to Lord Rawthorne's guests, she knew that there was something evil about him, just as she was sure that a great number of those present were prepared not only to tolerate the Thugs but perhaps even to encourage them.

It took away all her joy in the barbarous splendour and beauty of the evening, and wherever she looked she could see only the little boy's face and the tears coming into his eyes when he had said:

"Mother dead."

It was with a sense of relief that Brucena realised Cousin William had indicated that his wife was tired and it was time to retire.

"There is no need for you to go," Lord Rawthorne said hastily as she rose.

"On the contrary," Brucena said coldly. "When Mrs. Sleeman leaves, I obviously must accompany her."

"Why?" he asked. "There are plenty of other people to chaperone you, if that is what you want."

She did not deign to answer him, but merely followed Amelie as she curtseyed to the Maharajah, and then, escorted by her husband, moved towards the door.

Everyone they passed put their palms together politely and bowed their heads, but, while they seemed respectful, Brucena somehow felt that the expression in their eyes belied it, and she was glad to be leaving the great chandeliered Hall in which the Maharajah had entertained them.

Perhaps, she thought, it was as glittering as its owner's jewels, but beneath it there was something dark and frightening and every instinct in her body shrank from it.

There was a carriage outside to carry them back to the guest-house, but only as they drove the short distance to it did Brucena realise that Major Huntley was not with them.

'I suppose he is enjoying the dancing girls,' she thought scornfully, then told herself that, in justice, he might have other reasons for staying.

It suddenly struck her that she had seen very little of him that evening.

He had been present at dinner, which had been a long-drawn-out feast, but she could not remember if afterwards he had sat beside them on the satin-covered chairs which were grouped round the inevitable gold throne which accommodated the Maharajah.

At the time, all she had been conscious of was Lord Rawthorne whispering compliments in her ears, making love to her with the brand of arrogance and impertinence that was peculiarly his own.

'I dislike him more every time we meet,' Brucena thought.

She had known, and been annoyed, that Amelie had been watching his overtures with pleasure, and she knew too that whatever she might say, the Frenchwoman was convinced that in her own interests she should marry such an important man.

They reached the guest-house and Amelie gave a little sigh.

"It was a very spectacular evening," she said, "but I must admit to feeling rather tired."

"Not too tired, my darling?" her husband asked.

"No, I am all right," Amelie replied, "but I shall be glad to be able to lie down."

"Will you forgive me if I go back for a little while to the party?" William Sleeman asked. "I know that otherwise we shall offend our host, who has certainly put himself out to amuse us."

"Do not be too long, dearest," Amelie said, "although I think I shall be asleep when you return."

"I will do my best not to wake you," William Sleeman promised.

He kissed his wife, said good-night to Brucena, and disappeared out into the night to where the carriage was still waiting for him.

Brucena looked after him, an expression of consternation on her face.

She had meant to take this opportunity of telling him about the small boy, but now it was impossible.

There had been no chance for her to do so on her previous return to the guest-house, for it was already getting late and she had to hurry to be ready at the time the carriage was to carry them to the Palace.

'I must tell him, I must!' she thought, but there was nothing she could do now but go to her own bedroom, where her maids were waiting for her.

They helped her out of her gown, and then she brushed her hair absent-mindedly, thinking of the child and feeling that even if Cousin William knew about him, there would be nothing he could do.

'It is an intolerable position,' she thought.

She was aware that in any other State, the Resident would allow a child who had been kidnapped in such a way to be taken back to the Province in which the crime had taken place.

Yet she knew without asking that Mr. Cavendish would do absolutely nothing to help Cousin William and instead would actively obstruct him from carrying out what he believed to be his duty.

'The whole situation is horrible!' Brucena thought.

The maids left her and she got into bed, but she found it impossible to sleep.

Then for the first time she thought that perhaps she had put herself in a dangerous position.

All she had done was give the little boy a tassel from her sunshade, but she had asked him about his mother, and she had a feeling that if he was questioned, there would be no reason for him not to tell the truth about what the English lady had said to him.

She had an uncomfortable feeling that the man whom she had seen advancing towards them would be well aware of who she was and where he had seen her before.

"He will know that I will tell Cousin William," she decided, "and he will be afraid that his crime will be discovered."

Then she told herself that he would not take it so seriously. Even if William Sleeman knew about him, as long as he remained in Gwalior he was safe.

She felt her mind going over and over everything that had happened, until she felt almost like a squirrel in a cage turning round and round and yet not advancing at all.

She had been lying there thinking for two or perhaps three hours—it might even have been longer —and now the shafts of moonlight were flooding in through the uncurtained windows, turning everything in the room to silver.

Looking at it from behind the mosquito-net, it seemed to Brucena strange, beautiful but at the same time sinister.

The moonlight itself was revealing, yet the shadows were very dark and so much was hidden.

Then suddenly there was a sound.

It was not very distinct, yet it was different from the other noises of the night that she had heard during the past few hours.

She could not explain why, but she knew it was different from the other sounds, which had become part of her thoughts and yet had not impinged upon them.

She suddenly felt herself shiver, and it was almost as if the base of her skull prickled with a fear that she had never felt before in her whole life.

She sat up in bed, listening, straining her ears, waiting for that sound again.

She was not even certain if it was a movement or a footfall or just something she sensed, and yet she could have sworn that it was caused by a human being.

It flashed through her mind that one means by which the man who had brought the little boy to Gwalior could avoid recognition as a Thug would be to kill her.

Even as she thought of it she told herself that she was being absurd.

Thugs only killed travellers. But to save himself might he not resort to murder?

She began to tremble, then little shivers of fear almost like streaks of lightning were running through her and she knew that she was desperately afraid as she had never been afraid before.

She heard the sound again and now she was almost certain that it was a footfall, hardly more than the ghost of one, and yet undoubtedly made by a man who was moving towards her ... threatening her ... menacing her. ...

For a moment it seemed as if it was impossible for her to move and that if she wished to run away her body would not obey the commands of her brain.

Then cautiously, moving silently so that she would not be heard, she lifted the mosquito-netting from the side of the bed farthest from the window and slipped out.

She felt the softness of a rug beneath her bare

feet, and then as she stood, hesitating, still listening, the sound came again.

Now with a terror that had no reason and a panic in which she could not even think clearly, she ran across the room, pulled open the door, and stepped into the darkness of the passage outside.

Vaguely she knew she must go for help, but to whom or where she had no idea.

Anywhere, so long as it was away from the horror of what frightened her, the murderer who, she was certain, intended to take her life.

The passage was in complete darkness, and as she started to run she crashed into someone large and massive, and at the sheer horror of it a scream rose in her throat.

She felt as if she had not run away from death but into it and now there was no hope, no chance of escape.

Because she was so frightened she could only tremble all over and wait to die.

Then two arms went round her and she knew by instinct, not thought, that she was safe.

She clung frantically to the man who was holding her, still trembling violently but at the same time knowing far away at the back of her mind that she was now safe from what she had feared.

"What is it?" a voice asked in so low a whisper that she could barely hear it.

Because she could not answer, her voice having died in her throat, she could only look up in the direction of where the voice had come from, and as she did so, a man's lips took possession of hers and held her captive.

For a moment she felt nothing, not even surprise, only a sudden sensation of relief that swept away the agonizing fear.

Then as the man's arms tightened, her lips were suddenly soft beneath the insistence of his, and she

felt the terror, which was still making her tremble,
dissolve as if the sun were rising in the darkness of
the sky.

Something warm and wonderful and infinitely
marvellous crept up her body, moving slowly and yet
relentlessly through her breasts, up to reach her con-
stricted throat, and from there into her lips.

It was so perfect, so unlike anything she had
ever felt or known before, and so rapturous, that she
felt her whole being surrender to the glory of it.

It was like touching the life-force itself and becoming a part of it, and she felt the wonder of it
seeping through her veins.

At the same time, she felt that she ceased to be
human and became Divine, for only gods could know
such rapture.

How long the kiss lasted Brucena had no idea;
she knew only that the darkness and terror had gone
and she was in a light which came from her heart
and was part of the beauty of music, flowers, and
sunshine.

She was safe as she had always wanted to be
and there was no more fear.

Iain Huntley raised his head and said in a voice
which was hard to recognise:

"My darling, my sweet! I have loved you for so
long and have not dared to tell you so."

"I ... love you, too," Brucena whispered, her
voice quivering, "but I had not ... realised it was ...
love."

Even as she spoke, she knew that this was why
she had disliked Lord Rawthorne, why she had hated
his compliments and had found him repulsive.

It was also why she had been angry at Iain
Huntley's disapproval and his habit of finding her in
compromising circumstances, and why she had
missed him when he had not been there.

It was now impossible to think but only to feel,

and without really meaning to she moved even closer to him.

Then he was kissing her again, kissing her with long, slow, passionate kisses that seemed to draw her very heart from her body and make it his.

He kissed her until the whole world seemed to turn upside-down and glisten and glitter with a radiance like the chandeliers in the Maharajah's Palace.

Then at length, as if human nature broke under the strain of such ecstasy, Brucena hid her face against his neck and he said very quietly:

"I love you, but you must tell me what has upset you."

It was then that Brucena realised she had forgotten why she had run from her bedroom, why she had been terror-stricken, and why she had sought safety only to find it in Iain Huntley's arms.

As it all came back to her she felt the shafts of fear run through her again, and she said hastily, her words tumbling over one another:

"I have . . . something very . . . important to . . . tell you."

"I am ready to listen," he said, "but not here. It would be best to go back to your room."

He felt her start at his decision, and he asked:

"Is there something there that has upset you?"

"Not . . . now that . . . you are with . . . me," she said after a pause.

With his arms round her, he drew her down the passage and opened her door.

Apprehensively Brucena looked round, half-fearing to see a figure near the window or a knife in the bed, but there was nothing. Nothing but the moonlight and the sheet crumpled and thrown back as she had left it.

Iain Huntley shut the door behind them, then asked:

"What has upset you, my precious?"

As he spoke, Brucena gave a little gasp, for he was not in the evening-dress of the Bengal Lancers as he had been when they dined with the Maharajah, but dressed as a native with a turban on his head and a white dhoti that made him appear like every other Indian.

He smiled at her astonishment and said:

"You have made me forget everything except that I love you."

"You have ... been out in ... disguise?"

He nodded, and said with a smile:

"At this moment we are neither of us our ordinary selves."

His words made Brucena suddenly conscious of her own appearance, and she was aware for the first time that she had nothing on but a thin lawn night-gown trimmed with lace.

Instinctively she put up her hands as if to protect herself from his gaze, and Iain Huntley said quietly:

"Get into bed, my precious. Then we will talk, although it may seem reprehensible, but I have to know what has frightened you."

"Yes ... of course," Brucena agreed.

She lifted up the mosquito-net to get back into bed, and would have slipped her legs under the sheet, but at that moment, to her surprise, Iain Huntley suddenly took her by the arm and pulled her roughly from the bed back onto the floor.

She gave a little murmur of astonishment and looked at him with wide eyes, but already he had bent forward under the mosquito-net and was turning back the sheet slowly and carefully.

She saw him pause, saw his hand go to his side, and the next moment he seemed to lurch forward.

"What ... is it? What ... are you ... doing?" she asked, her voice a terrified whisper.

Then as she moved sideways she saw that in one

hand he held a long, pointed knife, and in the other was something small and green, which moved only with the last contraction of its muscles in death.

For a moment it was impossible to move. Then as she pressed her hands against her breasts in sheer horror, Iain carried the snake across the room to the window and threw it out.

"A snake!" Brucena exclaimed. "Then... there was... something! I knew... he... I am sure... he was... trying to... kill me!"

"But who? And why?" Iain asked, turning from the window.

She saw the knife disappear back into his clothing.

"Why you, my precious?"

"That is... what I want to... tell you," Brucena said. "Oh, Iain... I am... frightened. Take me... away."

As she spoke she ran towards him and his arms went round her again.

Holding her close, feeling her heart thumping tumultuously against his, he knew that she was obsessed with a terror that made it almost impossible for her to speak.

"It is all right," he said gently. "You are safe. I will look after you, and there will be no more snakes—that I promise you!"

"He will... try again to kill me," Brucena said, her voice coming as if from a long distance. "He knew I had... recognised the boy."

"What are you talking about?" Iain asked.

Then he said:

"You will not want to sleep here, that I understand. I will find you another room, and you shall tell me all about it, but first—"

He looked round indecisively before, to Brucena's surprise, he took his arms from her and sat her down gently on a chair.

He pulled the turban from his head and, walking

across the bedroom, entered the adjoining wash-room.

It was fairly primitive, with a sluice, several cans of cold water, and a tank attached to the wall, making a kind of shower.

As Brucena waited, shaken and frightened, not knowing what he was doing, Iain came back wearing one of the towelling-robes which were to be found in all the wash-places.

They were provided so that anyone who had used the shower could dry in comfort without even bothering to rub themselves down.

Iain, without his native dress, now looked like an ordinary Englishman and there was nothing to show that when Brucena had run into him in the passage, he had been disguised as a native.

He looked round her bedroom, picked up a negligé which the maids had left hanging over a chair, and said:

"Put this on, my darling. I am going to find another bedroom for you, but before I fetch a servant, you must tell me what frightened you and why in God's name there should be a snake in your bed."

Brucena looked up at him, then rose to her feet and moved close into his arms.

"Hold . . . me! Hold me . . . close to you," she said. "I am . . . frightened! If it was not a snake it could have been a knife, or a . . . yellow . . . scarf!"

Her voice broke on the last words and Iain said reassuringly:

"The Thugs would not touch you, my darling. Why should they?"

"That is . . . what I am . . . going to tell . . . you."

She gave a little sigh.

"I wanted to tell Cousin William tonight . . . but he went back to the party and I knew I must not speak to him when Amelie was . . . there."

"Tell me," Iain said.

He sat down on a chair, and as he did so, he

pulled her down onto his knee, cradling her in his arms as if she were a child.

She put her head on his shoulder so that she could talk very softly.

Because it was wonderful to be so close to him and to know for the moment that nothing could hurt her, she was able to tell him fairly coherently of the little boy who had given her the flower and to whom in return she had given the ball of pink silk.

She went on to explain how she had seen the child again in tears as they had driven back to Saugor and how she had been sure that the Thugs had killed his family.

She paused for breath before she told Iain how the boy's unhappy little face had haunted her and she had been convinced that he was somewhere in Gwalior.

"I was right," she murmured, "and, oh, Iain... what will happen to him... with those terrible men ... what will they do ... to him?"

"Finish your story, my darling," he said quietly.

She felt him stiffen as her tale progressed from her seeing and talking again to the boy that afternoon until the moment when she had heard strange sounds and been terrified that the man who had seen her talking to the boy was coming to kill her.

"That is ... what he ... meant to do," she said in a broken voice.

"It is something he will not do again," Iain said. "I am going to find another room for you, my darling. I want you to try to sleep. Everything will be all right—that I promise you. I only wish you had told me before."

"I was afraid you would think I was only... imagining things," Brucena replied. "You were so determined to tell me ... nothing about the... Thugs."

"Do you know why?"

"No."

"Because you were so beautiful, so young, so unspoilt. I could not bear you to hear such tales of horror and degradation. I wanted you to remain just as you were when you arrived, looking at India with an awe and a wonder as if it were a Kingdom of light and sunshine."

"To me that is what it still is," Brucena said, "and ... it is even more ... wonderful now ... because I have found ... you."

He did not speak and after a moment she asked:

"You do love me? You really do ... love me?"

"It is impossible to tell you how much," Iain replied.

There was a faint smile on his lips as he went on:

"I fought against my feelings at first, telling myself I was too old, too dedicated to my profession. But, my precious, I find it impossible to fight against love."

"I knew it would be like this when I found ... love, but Amelie kept telling me that I must marry ... Lord Rawthorne. I know now the reason why I hated him was because I was already, although I was unaware of it ... in love with ... you."

"You are sure of that?" Iain asked.

"Quite ... quite sure!"

She looked up at him and in the moonlight he could see the expression on her face, and he knew that if she had been beautiful before, love had given her a radiance that was indescribable.

As if he could not help himself, he was kissing her again, kissing her demandingly, possessively, until she quivered against him and her breath came quickly between her lips.

"I love you!" he said, his voice unsteady. "But, my darling, I must protect you not only against the Thugs and murderers by whom we are surrounded, but also against any gossip. If anyone should see us at the moment, we would be considered very reprehensible!"

"I do not . . . care what anyone . . . thinks or says," Brucena said. "You love me, and that is all that . . . matters."

"All that will ever matter," Iain replied, "but I want you to get some sleep."

He put her feet on the ground and stood up.

"Now," he said, "I want you to stand just inside the door, looking frightened, while I fetch the servants."

"You will not . . . leave me alone . . . for long?"

"I am only going into the Hall," he replied, "where I know there are servants on duty."

He kissed her again swiftly, then as she stood by the open door he hurried down the passage, shouting.

A few seconds later he came back with several of the servants, looking as if they had been aroused from sleep.

"I heard the Mem Sahib scream," Iain was explaining, "and she told me she had seen a snake crawling on her bed. I killed it and threw it out the window. You will find it on the verandah."

One of the servants went to the window and looked out.

"It is a dangerous one, Sahib," he said. "Very dangerous!"

"I was aware of that," Iain said briefly. "And we must find the Mem Sahib another room. She cannot sleep here tonight."

"No, of course not, Sahib. There is a room two doors away that is unoccupied."

"You will search it," Iain said firmly. "Search it carefully, for His Highness will be extremely angry that one of his guests has been frightened in such a way."

This had the effect he intended, and the servants scuttled off. By the time Brucena, walking slowly with Iain at her side, reached the empty bedroom she was sure that they had searched every inch of it.

The room was very much the same as the one she had just vacated, and as the servants filed away, salaaming as they did so, she asked:

"What are you . . . going to do?"

"I will tell you that later," he said. "Do not forget that in the morning you must show yourself extremely upset by what has occurred, and I think you should be prepared to leave immediately after breakfast. I am going to wake your cousin now and tell him why you should go."

"Do not upset Amelie," Brucena said quickly.

"She will know nothing except that you have been frightened by a snake," Iain replied. "Leave everything else to me."

He held her hand very tightly and his eyes were on her lips.

She thought he would kiss her, but then she realised that the servants were just outside the door.

"Thank . . . you," she said softly.

"I love you!" he replied.

But he was saying more with his eyes than he said with his lips.

When Brucena was alone, because she was so happy she knew that nothing mattered except that Iain loved her.

She heard his voice in the distance and knew that there were servants now on guard outside her window, and she guessed too that there would be servants sleeping in the passage outside her door, as there had been on their way to Gwalior.

Now she was no longer afraid of being murdered, for she knew confidently that Iain would look after her.

As she fell asleep she found herself repeating his name over and over again as if it were a talisman.

* * *

Brucena was not surprised, after what Iain had said, that when she came out to the covered verandah where breakfast was laid, Cousin William said:

"I am very upset to hear, Brucena, that you were frightened by a snake last night. I thought myself that all this bougainvillaea and other shrubs had been planted far too near to the houses. If I lived here, I would have them cut back to at least thirty feet from the buildings."

"I think that would be sacrilege where the crimson bougainvillaea is concerned," Brucena replied, "but quite frankly, Cousin William, I am terrified of snakes!"

"We all are, but Huntley tells me you were very brave," he replied. "Nevertheless, I think it is time we left, and Amelie is already having her things packed. I will send a servant to tell your maids to do the same."

Amelie had not appeared at breakfast, but it was impossible to talk openly to Cousin William because there were always servants in the room.

It was, however, very early, and Brucena thought there would be plenty of time for them to pack, say good-bye to Lord Rawthorne, and be on their way before it became unpleasantly hot.

She was not surprised when a short time later Lord Rawthorne strode onto the verandah, obviously incensed at their decision to depart.

He was frowning and he seemed to be, Brucena thought, like a typhoon.

"What is all this, Sleeman?" he enquired, his voice rising. "I have been told you are leaving."

"We have enjoyed our visit enormously," William Sleeman replied, "but Your Lordship will understand that I cannot take leave of absence for long from my own Province."

"But I expected you to stay for at least a week."

"That is what we would have liked to do," William Sleeman said, "but I have in fact had a messenger from Saugor, telling me that there is trouble in the South and I am therefore required at home to deal with it."

"Surely you can delegate authority better than that?" Lord Rawthorne asked angrily. "No-one is indispensable."

"That is what I have always believed myself," William Sleeman replied, "but apparently in this instance I am, not only as Superintendent, but also as Magistrate and as District Officer. I wear so many hats that when I am not there, they actually miss me!"

He spoke jovially, but Lord Rawthorne asked sulkily:

"I suppose you would not leave your wife and Miss Nairn behind?"

"I am afraid not," William Sleeman replied. "To begin with, my wife, as you know, is not in a condition to be left anywhere without me, and Brucena is not only essential for her comfort, she is in our charge and far too precious to leave lying about!"

William Sleeman was making a joke of it, but Brucena was quite certain that he intended to be very firm and nothing Lord Rawthorne might say would divert him from his intention to go home.

Finally, a little later than they had intended, they started off, Lord Rawthorne glowering but riding as their escort.

With a posse of the Gwalior Cavalry beside their own, and the cheers of the populace, it was quite an impressive departure.

There were, however, no kettle-drums or trumpets, and as they drove away with the red Fort behind them, Brucena felt that Cousin William heaved a sigh of relief, as she did.

She felt worried that there was no sign of Iain. She kept looking for him amongst the mounted soldiers riding behind them, and only when she could bear it no longer did she ask:

"Is Major Huntley not coming with us?"

"He has gone shooting," William Sleeman replied. "He agreed to do so yesterday, and he did not wish to disappoint those who had made the arrangements."

Brucena drew in her breath, but with Lord Rawthorne riding beside the carriage, she did not want to say any more.

A few miles out of Gwalior the horses were brought to a standstill and they stopped to say good-bye to their host.

"It has been an extremely pleasant visit, Lord Rawthorne," Amelie said, holding up her hand. "I am only so sorry we could not stay longer."

"So am I!" Lord Rawthorne replied. "May I hope that you will permit me to stay with you again very shortly? I should think in about a week's time."

There was just a little pause before Amelie repeated:

"In a week, Lord Rawthorne?"

"I intend to continue my tour, which I interrupted when I reached Saugor and asked you to be my guests here in Gwalior."

He smiled and was looking at Brucena as he went on:

"As I told you then, I have friends in Bhopal and several other places which I wish to visit. So I plan to set off once again as an explorer of India, and I hope you will be as kind to me as you were on my last visit."

"Yes, yes, of course," Amelie said. "We shall look forward to it."

"I hope you will say the same," Lord Rawthorne said to Brucena.

Because she thought there was no point in being disagreeable, she answered:

"I only hope we shall be home by then."

"I am always prepared to wait," Lord Rawthorne said.

There was no doubt that there was a deeper meaning behind his words, which Brucena had no difficulty in understanding.

She wanted to reply: "If you waited until Doomsday it would make no difference!" Instead, she forced a smile to her lips.

Only when they drove on, with Lord Rawthorne watching them recede into the distance, did she say almost frantically to her cousin:

"Where is Iain? Why is he not with us?"

As she spoke, she knew that the use of Major Huntley's Christian name and the agitation in her voice made both William Sleeman and his wife stare at her in astonishment.

Then as the colour rose in her cheeks, her cousin said with a smile on his lips:

"So that is the way the wind blows! I must admit, Brucena, you have taken me by surprise!"

Brucena's cheeks were crimson as she said:

"I did not intend you to . . . know so . . . soon, but I cannot . . . bear to think that he is left . . . behind in that . . . place."

"Huntley can look after himself," William Sleeman said soothingly, but Amelie gave a little cry.

"Oh, Brucena, I did so want you to be 'My Lady'!"

"If you want my opinion," her husband said, "Brucena has made entirely the right decision. Huntley is worth a dozen of any self-opinionated Lords like Rawthorne, and what is more, he will go far on his own initiative."

Amelie was not listening; she was looking at Brucena as she said:

"Dearest, you know that all we really want is for you to be happy."

"I am happy . . . very, very happy," Brucena said, "but I . . . wish he were . . . here."

"Now stop worrying about him," William Sleeman said, "and be careful what you say—the servants have ears! Do not forget—he is tiger-shooting."

Brucena's eyes widened.

"You mean . . . ?" she began.

"I mean that if you are to be Iain's wife, you must learn to keep your mouth shut and know when to assume a poker-face."

"Yes . . . yes . . . of course," Brucena said humbly. "I am sorry I have been so . . . stupid."

At the same time, she knew that she was frantic with fear in case anything should happen to Iain.

How could her cousin leave him alone in Gwalior with all those Thugs? Men only too willing to strangle him with a yellow scarf, put snakes in his bed, or murder him in any way which occurred to them at the moment!

They stayed the night in a Dak bungalow in the Gwalior Province. Brucena found it difficult to sleep and lay awake praying that Iain would be safe and that she would soon be in his arms again.

As every moment passed, she felt that her love for him increased. He seemed now to fill her whole world and there was nothing but him.

Even the beauty of India had ceased to move her, and all she could think about was his voice, the safety of his arms, and his lips on hers.

When they drove on the next day she could not imagine how her cousin and Amelie could seem so unconcerned when she felt herself growing more tense and more worried every mile they moved farther away from Gwalior with no sign of the man she loved.

'I always thought love must be a happy state to be in,' she thought to herself, 'but this is an agony worse than any physical pain, because my heart can suffer far more than my body.'

They reached the boundary of Gwalior State, and the gorges and hills were now left behind. Now everything was flatter, except that there were more mango groves and soon they would come to the sugarcane which Cousin William had planted.

Just over the border there was a Dak bungalow more comfortable than most of those at which they had spent a night on their way to Gwalior. Here, to Brucena's surprise, they were to stay longer.

William Sleeman explained that he had a number of officials to see and he also wished to inspect the boundary between the two Provinces.

Brucena was quite certain that this concerned the Thugs, but it did not make it any easier not to worry ceaselessly because Iain had been left behind and there was still no sign of him.

Amelie was quite content to rest for a few days, not rising until it was nearly luncheon-time, and then sitting on the verandah, out of ear-shot of her husband, who was entertaining local dignitaries, but glad that he was near her.

Brucena rode with two Cavalrymen in attendance when Cousin William could not accompany her, then when it was cool she would walk restlessly up and down the road outside the Dak bungalow, looking always in the direction of Gwalior and wondering what was happening as the days passed and there was still no news of Iain.

Surely, she told herself angrily, Cousin William should have left at least two Sepoys with him.

Then she knew, without having to be told, that Iain was working in disguise.

She was aware that the invitation to shoot was just an excuse to stay behind. At the same time, she could not bear to think of him disguised as an Indian amongst the crowds in the old town of Gwalior.

What would happen if he was discovered?

She felt almost sick with worry, and at the same time it was impossible to stop herself from thinking of and praying for him every minute of the day and night.

She told herself she must trust him to return safely, as obviously William Sleeman did.

But there were so many things that might go wrong! What did it matter, she asked herself, if the Thugs flourished and multiplied a thousandfold as long as Iain was safe?

Cousin William might have dedicated himself to the suppression of Thuggee, but she was concerned only with the safety of one man—the man she loved.

* * *

They had now stayed four days at the Dak bungalow, and since Cousin William and Amelie had given no signs of continuing their journey, Brucena, feeling that she would go insane if she was inactive, walked determinedly out onto the road.

"Where are you going, dearest?" asked Amelie, who was sitting in the shade of the verandah.

"For a walk," Brucena replied.

"You must not go out of sight," Amelie said.

"I have to go somewhere," Brucena replied. "Being cooped up here, thinking and worrying, is driving me crazy!"

"I am so sorry, dearest, but he will be all right, I promise you!"

"How can you know?" Brucena enquired. "How can you have any idea of what may be happening to him? If he does not come soon, I shall go and look for him."

"Do you think you would recognise him?" Amelie asked quietly.

"I should recognise him anywhere. I should know instinctively that he was there," Brucena said.

She felt the tears come into her eyes as she

spoke, and because she was a little ashamed of them, she began to walk along the dusty road.

"Do not go too far," Amelie warned, "or I shall send a Sepoy after you."

Because she was angry, Brucena merely tossed her head and walked on.

She had not bothered to put on a hat, as no-one would see her, but she carried her sunshade to protect her from the sun, which had lost much of its strength as it was getting late in the day.

The road, long and dusty, stretched away into the distance, and she thought that perhaps Iain was at this moment in prison in Gwalior, perhaps being tortured to make him reveal the secrets that he knew about the Thugs.

If he was, what could anyone do? And if they could not rescue him, then he would die, as so many men had died in the service of India.

"It is not worth it! It is not worth it!" Brucena cried in her heart.

But she knew that to men like Cousin William and Iain, India was worth every sacrifice it demanded of them, even if it meant giving their very life for it.

"I have no answer to that," Brucena told herself.

She realised that, deep in her thoughts, she had walked quite a little way from the bungalow, and now because she did not wish to upset or worry Amelie she must turn back.

She looked towards Gwalior and sent out a prayer for Iain's safety.

"Take care of him, God, and bring him back to me," she prayed. "I love him, and without him there would be nothing left in my life except emptiness. Keep him safe, O God, keep him safe!"

The tears were back in her eyes with the intensity of her feelings.

Then as she was turning back resolutely in the direction of the Dak bungalow, she saw, coming down the side of a small incline where there were a few scraggy trees, a man and a child driving in front of them a goat.

It was a large she-goat with its udders full of milk, and it was moving slowly and reluctantly, as if it had no wish to go any farther.

Brucena looked at it perfunctorily before glancing at the man, who was wearing a dirty, torn dhoti, then at the child.

Quite suddenly she stood very still.

The little boy was in rags, but there was no mistaking that small, beautiful face or the huge, long-lashed eyes.

For a moment she thought that she must be dreaming, that her imagination had distorted her vision. Then she looked again at the man in the dirty dhoti and gave a little cry of joy that seemed to be carried on the evening air.

She started to run towards them.

Chapter Six

"You are . . . safe! You are . . . safe!"

That evening Brucena said over and over again the same words which she had cried when she had run towards Iain and, regardless of his appearance, flung her arms round his neck.

He looked into her eyes and she never noticed the dirt on his darkened skin or the ragged condition of his clothes.

All she knew was that he had come back to her and nothing else in the whole world mattered.

"I am safe," he said quietly. "I told you to trust me."

"I was . . . frightened . . . so very frightened! But you have . . . brought the little boy back with you. How . . . did you . . . manage it?"

She looked down at her small friend as she spoke, and he had the same smile on his lips that he had given her the first time they met.

"His name is Azim," Iain said, "and he is very tired. We have walked a long way and very quickly."

"But the she-goat protected you," Brucena said in a low voice.

"I can see you are very knowledgeable," he replied, "but I think we should go to a place of safety as soon as possible, and . . ."

Before he could say any more, Brucena gave a little cry.

"You ... mean they are ... following you?"

"I hope not," he answered, "but I never believe in taking chances."

"Cousin William and Amelie are at the Dak bungalow," Brucena explained. "Let us go there at once."

They moved forward, a strange party, Brucena in her pretty light gown, Iain and the child looking like the poorest beggars, and the goat driven relentlessly forward when all she wanted to do was lie down.

Azim was given into the care of Cousin William's personal servant, Nasir, who had been with him for many years, and as Iain disappeared to wash and change, Brucena sat down beside Amelie to tell her how frightened she had been.

"It is indeed frightening, *ma pauvre petite*," Amelie agreed, "but William gets upset if I worry about him too much, and you will have to hide your feelings as I have learnt to do ever since we were married."

"It is agonising to feel that someone you love is in danger and you can do nothing about it," Brucena said in a low voice.

"*C'est l'amour*," Amelie said with a smile. "Love is wonderful, but it can also be extremely painful."

"That is what I have found," Brucena agreed.

She wondered how much agony the future held for her if she was always to be apprehensive every time Iain was away from her.

But when he came out onto the verandah wearing his uniform and looking conventionally English, it was impossible to think that she had seen him, only a short time before, looking like the lowest-caste Hindu.

And she knew, when her eyes met his, that any suffering was worthwhile so long as he loved her.

After a dinner which Iain made amusing by telling them in the most light-hearted way of his and Azim's adventures on their journey from Gwalior to the border, the servants cleared the table and left.

As Amelie also went from the room and her husband followed her, Brucena said in a low voice:

"Tell me what . . . really happened."

Iain moved to sit beside her and took her hand in his.

"I am not being unkind, my precious," he said, "when I tell you that I never talk about my exploits once they are over. It is not that I do not trust you. It is just that in this campaign in which your cousin and I are engaged, there are so many things that are best left unsaid."

"But I want to know," Brucena persisted. "How did you get Azim away? Surely the man who kidnapped him and tried to . . . kill me . . . attempted to prevent you from . . . taking him?"

Iain was silent for a moment, then he said:

"Let me set your mind at rest by telling you that he is not in a position to frighten you again—ever!"

"You mean . . . he is dead?"

"Yes."

Iain said the monosyllable reluctantly and Brucena gave a little cry.

"You killed him! I am glad! At least he will no longer abduct little boys and murder their mothers."

"You are sounding very blood-thirsty, my dear," William Sleeman remarked.

He had come back into the room without Brucena being aware of it, and she gave a little start as he spoke.

"I am sure Iain is telling you that which is best forgotten."

Brucena thought there was a note of reproof in her cousin's voice, and she said quickly:

"That is exactly what Iain was saying. But you can understand that I am very curious."

"An emotion which should certainly be discouraged where we are concerned," William Sleeman said. "I want to talk to Iain and I am going to give you exactly twenty minutes alone with him. Then I suggest, my dear, that you go to bed."

"Oh, Cousin William! That is not fair!" Brucena objected. "Twenty minutes when I have waited four days . . . or is it four centuries . . . for him!"

"Twenty minutes!" William Sleeman said firmly, and left them alone.

Brucena turned to Iain, a question on her lips.

He took her in his arms, drew her close, and said:

"Why waste time in talking when I want to kiss you more than I have ever wanted anything in my whole life?"

Before she could reply, he kissed her until everything seemed to disappear but him.

She felt as if again he carried her into the sunshine and the light and they were both enveloped in the glory that was part of the Divine.

She no longer felt human, afraid or anxious, she only knew that with Iain's arms round her she was immortal and so was he.

In her heart was a rapture that was so spiritual, so perfect, that they themselves were part of the perfection of it.

Only when Iain raised his lips from hers did Brucena say, her voice seeming to come from a very long way away:

"I . . . love you! I love you . . . and I still cannot . . . believe this has happened to me so . . . suddenly."

"I found myself thinking the same thing the last few days," Iain said. "And yet as Azim and I climbed cliffs, forded rivers, and hid at night in mango groves, I felt all the time that you were beside me, guiding me, helping me, and however dangerous anything was, we passed through it because you were there."

"Did you . . . really feel . . . like that?"

"It is impossible to explain what a difference you have made to me," he said. "Always before I have been very much alone, and I believed that was how I wanted my life to be—self-sufficient, dependent on nothing and nobody but myself. Now everything has changed because I met one beautiful young woman who looked at me with angry eyes."

"I was angry," Brucena admitted, "but it did not last. I wanted you to . . . approve of me."

"Now you know I not only approve but think you are the most wonderful person that ever existed," Iain said, "and there need be no more misunderstandings between us."

"How could there be?" Brucena asked. "Please . . . please . . . take care of yourself. If anything . . . happened to . . . you . . ."

She gave a little shudder.

"You have to learn to trust me," he said.

"You know I . . . want to do . . . that, but it is very . . . . difficult when I am so . . . . afraid for you."

He kissed her and she was able to say no more. Then reluctantly he took his arms from her and said:

"My Commanding Officer is waiting for me."

"It is unfair of William to take you away."

"I think he has something important to tell me, and I have many things to tell him," Iain said. "You will have to learn to be a soldier's wife, my darling."

He pulled her back into his arms; and a little later, thinking over what he had said, Brucena felt that Iain had spoken seriously and with intent.

As a soldier's wife she had to learn that his duty came first.

*   *   *

Lying in the small, narrow *karpoy*, or native bed, in a room that was little more than a square wooden box, Brucena told herself that although she might protest, she was only too willing to do anything that was required so long as she could be married to Iain.

She had often thought of the man she might marry, but always he had been anonymous, a blank face even in her imagination.

Now Iain filled her world. She knew that her dreams had come true and all her ideals had materialised in one man.

'I must have known instinctively that he was somewhere in the world waiting for me,' she told herself, 'and that was why I could never contemplate even for a moment, whatever Amelie might have said, marrying Lord Rawthorne or anyone like him. I suppose in my heart I have never wanted position or power or wealth, and I have always known that love was the only thing worth having.'

She thought that William would have said it was part of her romantic Cornish blood and the fairy-stories of Cornish heroes that her mother had told her when she was a little girl.

Deep in her subconscious they had remained, so that the men she met and the man she thought she might meet sometime in her life were measured against the Knights, the Saints, and the warring Kings who were part of Cornish history.

'I suppose one day,' she thought, 'Cousin William will be considered a hero for what he has done for the suppression of Thuggee, but perhaps Iain will play another part in the development of India.'

She was wondering what that could be, when she fell asleep, and when she next opened her eyes it was morning.

She sprang out of bed quickly because she knew that the quicker she dressed the sooner she would see Iain, and she wanted that more than anything else.

Now that he had joined them, they set off to Saugor as soon as it was possible.

When they reached the white bungalow surrounded with its flowers, to be greeted by the smiles and salaams of the servants, Brucena felt that it really was like coming home.

Nasir, Cousin William's servant, had already suggested that the cook at the bungalow would, he was sure, be happy to adopt Azim.

Apparently he was very devoted to his wife, who had given him two sons and three daughters, all of whom were now old enough to leave home.

"She is still a young woman," Nasir had said, "but she can have no more children. It is a great sadness."

"I will certainly talk to them about it," William Sleeman promised. "I like them both and think Azim would be very happy with them."

Brucena felt almost wistfully that he was such a dear little boy that she would like to adopt him herself. But she knew such an idea would present innumerable difficulties and she was wise enough to know that he would be happiest with people of his own caste.

He had enjoyed the journey back to Saugor because not only did he not have to talk—although Brucena had discovered that in fact Iain had carried him a great part of the way from Gwalior—but he was allowed to sit on the box of their carriage, where he could watch the coachman drive.

This not only delighted the child but left them with more room in the carriage for Amelie.

Brucena also helped solve this problem by saying she would like above all else to ride as Iain intended to do.

A horse was found for her and they rode either beside the carriage, to keep out the dust, or a little ahead of it, while the detachment of Cavalry rode behind them.

When they arrived, even though it had been a joy to ride with Iain, Brucena was glad to be back.

Her own comfortable bedroom seemed very attractive after the austerity of the Dak bungalows, and the maid who always attended her had everything

ready, including a bath, which was a luxury that was
not afforded to travellers.

Wearing one of her prettiest gowns, she went
into the Sitting-Room, excited at the thought of
being with Iain, and having learnt that Amelie did
not intend to join them at dinner but had retired
to bed.

To her joy, Iain was alone in the Sitting-Room,
looking extremely smart in the evening-clothes of the
Bengal Lancers, and when his eyes met hers, she
could not stop herself from running towards him.

He put his hands on her shoulders and held her at
arm's length, saying as he did so:

"You look very beautiful, my darling, but then
you always do!"

"I hope you will always think so," Brucena said.
"And shall I tell you how handsome I think you
are, or will you grow conceited?"

"I am the most conceited man in the world
because you love me," Iain answered.

As he spoke, he pulled her close against him
and she lifted her face to his, longing for the touch
of his lips on hers.

He looked down at her for a long moment before he kissed her with long, slow, passionate kisses
which made her heart beat tumultuously.

She wanted to be close to him, for him to go
on kissing her, but to her surprise he took his arms
from her and drew her to the sofa.

As they sat down he said:

"I have something to tell you, my darling."

"What is it?"

She knew by his tone that it was something
serious and she felt some of the rapture that his
kisses had evoked in her ebb away as if she had
been touched by a cold wind.

"Early tomorrow morning," Iain said quietly,
"your cousin and I have to leave."

"To . . . leave?" Brucena repeated. "But you have only just . . . returned. You cannot go . . . away so . . . . soon!"

'We have to."

"Why? Why? Surely Cousin William understands that you need rest?"

Iain looked away from her and she knew that he was choosing his words, wondering how much he could tell her.

Then, perceptively, because they were so close she could almost read his thoughts, she said:

"It has something to do with the Thugs. Something you found out when you were in Gwalior."

"I do not want you to ask questions."

"I have to know! That is the truth, is it not?" Brucena persisted. "You brought Cousin William some information that is valuable and he has to act on it at once."

Iain smiled.

"You are not only beautiful but very intelligent, my darling—something which one day I may find of great use to me. But now I just want you to trust me."

"Then trust me," Brucena said. "And tell me!"

"If I did that, I would be betraying secrets that are not mine alone," Iain answered. "I can only tell you that it is of great importance that we should act at once, and I must leave you to imagine the rest."

With superhuman effort Brucena bit back the protests which rose to her lips.

She was sure, without Iain filling in the details, that when in disguise in Gwalior he had discovered the whereabouts of a number of Thugs who were still in their own territory.

It was obvious that they must be caught before they could murder any more unsuspecting travellers, and to delay might give them a chance to escape to Gwalior, where neither Iain nor Cousin William could follow them.

Because she loved Iain and wanted to please him, Brucena forced herself to say:

"I ... understand."

Iain's expression was very tender as he replied:

"I knew I could rely on you, and when this is over and I come back, I promise you the first thing we are going to do, you and I, is to plan our wedding. I do not intend to wait long for you to become my wife."

He saw the light that came into Brucena's eyes and thought that no woman could look more radiant or more enchanting.

Then he kissed her until they heard footsteps outside the door and William Sleeman came in, dressed for dinner.

* * *

Brucena was awake before dawn broke, but because they had said good-bye the night before, she did not leave her room when she heard Iain and Cousin William ride off the following morning.

She had known how serious their mission was when they took all the available mounted irregulars with them, leaving behind to guard the bungalow only four Sepoy infantry-men in the charge of a Corporal.

When her father in Scotland had told her about what he had called "Cousin William's private Army," Brucena had thought it must be a very adequate force.

On arrival in India, however, Brucena had learnt that the area under his jurisdiction was twice as large as England, Scotland, and Wales combined.

Now she told herself miserably that he and Iain had not nearly enough men with them with which to destroy a hostile force.

Supposing the Thugs outnumbered them to such an extent that they were all killed in the conflict?

The mere idea of Iain being strangled by a yellow scarf, and then disappearing, never to be found or heard of again, was a horror that seemed to impinge on Brucena so vividly that she wanted to scream and run from her bedroom and beg Iain not to leave her.

Yet she knew that he would be shocked by and contemptuous of such weakness, so instead she lay in bed listening for the sounds of his departure, her fists clenched so tightly that her nails hurt the palms of her hands.

There was the jingle of the harness, the sounds of fidgeting hoofs on the hard ground, and a number of low-voiced commands. Then she guessed that the moment had come when Cousin William and Iain walked from the bungalow to mount their horses.

There was the first light of dawn on the eastern horizon, while the last glimmer of the evening stars were fading into the sable darkness. Then they were riding away and she listened until finally there was silence except for the crow of a cock as the day broke.

*   *   *

"Do not look so worried, *ma cherie*," Amelie admonished later in the morning.

The sun was beginning to grow strong and the gardeners were spraying the grass and flowers with water.

"How can you be so calm and unperturbed?" Brucena asked resentfully.

"My William is a very clever man," Amelie replied in French, "and Iain Huntley is clever too. They have already outwitted, arrested, or exterminated hundreds of Thugs, and I cannot believe that this expedition will be any different from the others."

Brucena gave a little laugh.

"The only difference is that I am involved in it now, and that, as far as I am concerned, makes it more terrifying and perhaps more important than any expeditions they have taken in the past."

"You will grow used to it," Amelie promised.

"I hope so."

But Brucena's tone of voice was not optimistic.

It took her thoughts off what might be happening to Iain when Azim came from the servants' quarters to bring her some flowers.

He handed them to her politely with a little bow that his new foster-parents must have taught him, and when she knelt down to put her arms round him, he smiled at her with the same entrancing expression which had attracted her the first day they had met.

"You are happy?" she asked him in Urdu.

He nodded, and brought out from some part of his new clothes the little ball of pink silk she had given him and a wooden whistle which Indians often carved for children.

He was obviously delighted with his possessions and showed them off, blowing the whistle at least a dozen times. Then, seeing one of the gardeners working below them, he ran from the verandah to show him his toys.

"He is a dear little boy," Brucena said.

"Having him here has made the cook's wife a very happy woman," Amelie replied. "She came to me in tears of joy this morning to tell me that because they now have Azim, her husband no longer wishes to take another wife."

"I should have thought that with the sons and daughters he has already, he has enough," Brucena remarked.

"A large family is a sign of prosperity," Amelie said, "and our cook is very conscious of his importance in being in William's employment."

Brucena laughed.

"Now I know that when I count the number of children my staff have, I shall be able to gauge Iain's social standing!"

"Perhaps one day you will have a Government House to administer," Amelie said, "and that means hundreds of servants at your command.'

"Are you still ambitious for me?" Brucena asked. "There is no need, Amelie. I am so happy that I could not be any happier if Iain were made Governor-General."

"I still hope that you will be 'My Lady' one way or another," Amelie said, as if she was determined to stick to her convictions.

Even as she spoke there was a sound of approaching horses, and as Brucena looked at Amelie, almost simultaneously their lips formed the same words:

"Lord Rawthorne!"

Brucena had in fact completely forgotten him and his promise to visit them.

In her anxiety over Iain and the joy of his safe return the previous evening, Lord Rawthorne, or anyone else for that matter, had ceased to exist.

Now round the corner of the drive came a carriage in which sat a familiar figure, and behind was an escort of Gwalior Cavalry.

'What a nuisance!' Brucena thought. 'Why does he have to turn up now? Especially with Cousin William away.'

She knew he would be difficult, and she wondered quickly whether it would be possible for both her and Amelie to retire to bed and have the servants tell him that they were indisposed.

Before she could come to any decision, it was far too late.

Lord Rawthorne had joined them on the verandah and was making himself what he believed to be agreeable, with his usual self-confidence combined with a touch of arrogance.

"I deeply regret, My Lord, that my husband has been called away and therefore cannot receive you," Amelie said.

"I am sorry to miss him," Lord Rawthorne replied, "but I am quite content to find that you and Miss Nairn are still here."

As he spoke, his eyes were on Brucena and it was quite obvious, without his saying so, that he was interested only in her presence.

She had feared that he would be difficult, and now she found that she was not mistaken.

He paid her fulsome compliments, regardless of the fact that Amelie was listening, and when they retired to dress for dinner Brucena said:

"For goodness' sake, do not leave me alone with him!"

"I think you would be wise to tell him that you are engaged," Amelie said. "That should at least dampen his ardour a little.'

"I doubt it, but I have every intention of doing so the moment the opportunity arises," Brucena replied.

She did not add that she was rather dreading the moment because she was not certain how Lord Rawthorne would react.

All through dinner he never took his eyes off her, and it was with the greatest difficulty that she managed to keep the conversation going between the three of them.

"We will leave you to your port, My Lord," Amelie said as the meal finished and she rose from the table.

However, Lord Rawthorne replied:

"I have no wish to be left alone. I will join you ladies in the Sitting-Room and drink my port there, although actually a glass of brandy would be more to my liking."

The head servant, who spoke and understood English, followed them into the Sitting-Room, carry-

ing a decanter of brandy which he set down beside
Lord Rawthorne's chair.

Brucena glanced at the clock, wondering for
how long they must make desultory conversation before she could say she wished to go to bed.

Then to Brucena's relief, Amelie decided, from
the expression in Lord Rawthorne's eyes as he looked
at Brucena, that the time had come to do something. Amelie said:

"It is at the moment a secret, My Lord, but I
feel that as you are a friend you would like to give
Brucena your good wishes, as she is engaged to be
married."

If she had intended to startle Lord Rawthorne,
she succeeded.

He stiffened, and there was an almost ferocious
note in his voice as he asked:

"Engaged to be married? To whom?"

"To Major Huntley," Amelie replied. "My husband is delighted that she should have found someone of whom we are both very fond."

"You are to marry Huntley?"

The question was directed at Brucena, and, feeling that his tone was impertinent, she raised her
chin as she replied:

"As Mrs. Sleeman says, for the moment it is a
secret, but we shall announce it as soon as I have
written to my father and Iain has informed his relatives."

"When was this arrangement made? Why did I
not know?"

The questions were sharp and seemed almost
to echo round the room.

Brucena contrived to look surprised as she replied:

"As you have just been informed, it was a
secret."

There was no doubt that Lord Rawthorne was
furious, and Brucena was thinking that this would

be a good time to retire, when a servant came into the room to speak in a low voice to Amelie.

She rose from her chair, saying:

"I will not be a moment, but there is a man who wishes to see William and in his absence I have to take a message."

She went from the room before Brucena had a chance to follow her.

The moment they were alone Lord Rawthorne said:

"It is intolerable! I have no intention of allowing you to marry Huntley!"

"I do not understand what you are saying," Brucena replied.

"You understand perfectly well," he answered. "You know that I fell in love with you the moment I saw you. It was only because you left Gwalior in such a hurry that I was not able to talk to you as I had intended to do."

"It is too late now to say anything that you might regret," Brucena murmured.

"I should certainly not regret anything I said to you," Lord Rawthorne said. "I understand now why you were keeping me at arm's length, but nothing has happened that is not irrevocable."

"Again, I do not understand what you are trying to say."

"Then let me spell it out to you," Lord Rawthorne said. "I want you and you will marry me!"

"That is certainly something you should not have said," Brucena replied. "I am engaged to Iain Huntley and I intend to marry him."

"And I tell you I will do everything to prevent it! Good God, can you really prefer that obscure, unimportant Thug-catcher to me?"

If he had not spoken so seriously and so violently, it might have been amusing, but as it was it flashed through Brucena's mind that he might in some way be able to hurt Iain.

If he was resentful, he might disparage him to his superior officers, and complaints from distinguished personages had, in the past, often been instrumental in ruining a man's career—her father had told her that.

It suddenly struck her that she must be very tactful in order to protect Iain, and she wished that Amelie had said nothing but had left Lord Rawthorne to find out later that she was not free.

However, the damage, if it was damage, was done, and she must now be clever enough to prevent His Lordship from taking revenge on the man she loved.

"I . . . I feel I should . . . . say," she said in a quiet, hesitating little voice, "how very . . . honoured I am that . . . Your Lordship should have thought of me in the . . . manner you are indicating . . . but it never struck me for . . . one moment . . . that that might be the case."

"You must have been aware of my intentions," he declared.

Brucena smiled.

"Your Lordship has a reputation, which you must know well, of being very successful as a . . . 'ladies' man.' I could not guess for one moment that where I was concerned you were . . . serious."

As she spoke, she knew that the flattery had to some extent alleviated his anger, and after a moment's pause he said:

"I admit that there has been a little gossip about me in the past, but I knew from the moment I saw you that you were different."

"How could I be?" Brucena asked, spreading out her hands in a helpless gesture.

"I would like to know the answer to that question myself," Lord Rawthorne said. "I only know that you attract me in a manner that is different from anything I have felt before. The more I see you, the more I fall in love with you."

He paused before he said:

"I meant to tell you the moment you came to Gwalior. I thought it would be very romantic there, perhaps in the exotic setting of His Highness's Palace. But you left with such precipitate haste that I had no chance to do anything but follow you."

"I am sorry . . . so very sorry," Brucena said.

"Are you sorry?"

There was a meaning she had not intended behind his question, and she said quickly:

"I am sorry you should have gone to so much trouble on my behalf. I would not wish you in any way to be unhappy."

"That is something I do not intend to be," he said with a sudden resolute note in his voice which frightened her.

Then to her relief Amelie came back into the room.

"It was nothing very important," she said. "Just a message I have to convey to my husband on his return."

She glanced from Brucena to Lord Rawthorne as she spoke, and she knew there was a feeling of tension in the air.

"I am sure, My Lord," she said, "that you would like to retire early tonight. Tomorrow, if you are still with us, I would be glad to give a dinner-party for you. We have various neighbours who I am sure would be very honoured to meet you."

"That would be delightful, Mrs. Sleeman," Lord Rawthorne replied.

But his eyes were on Brucena as he spoke, and both she and Amelie knew that his thoughts were elsewhere.

They said their good-nights and went to their own rooms.

Brucena did not undress immediately because she felt worried and anxious, thinking that Amelie had perhaps done the wrong thing in telling Lord Rawthorne about her engagement to Iain.

She wondered how she could persuade him not to be so angry and bitter that he would make trouble.

'He is a very unpredictable man and I feel in some ways a dangerous one,' she thought to herself.

She felt so agitated that she did not call her maid but went out through her bedroom window onto the verandah.

It was separate from the verandah in the front of the bungalow, on which they usually sat, and was on the side of the house, running along the east wall.

Brucena walked on the wooden boards in her satin evening-slippers which made no sound. As she reached the far end of the verandah where it ended against the north wall of the bungalow, she heard Lord Rawthorne's voice.

It surprised her because she thought he would be in the front of the house, where his bedroom was situated.

Then she heard him say:

"I understand that I must congratulate you on the splendid way you have assisted Captain Sleeman in his gigantic task of suppressing the Thugs."

A man's voice replied, but Brucena could not hear exactly what he said, and she wondered who was speaking, until Lord Rawthorne went on:

"It is obvious that you will not be a Corporal for long. Do you enjoy being in the Army?"

"Yes, Lord Sahib. It is very interesting."

Now Brucena knew to whom Lord Rawthorne was speaking. It was the Corporal who had been left in charge of the Sepoys.

She knew him to be a keen young Indian who William had said would look after them well in his absence.

"I admire Captain Sleeman very much indeed!" Lord Rawthorne continued. "I know everyone; including the Governor-General, is very impressed with what he and his men like you have achieved in this neighbourhood."

Brucena was amazed as she listened.

Why was Lord Rawthorne making such a fuss of the Corporal?

It seemed strangely out-of-character.

She had noticed when they were at Gwalior that he treated the native servants as if they had no importance as individuals and were there only to obey his orders.

"You must be sorry to miss this expedition on which Captain Sleeman has just gone," Lord Rawthorne was saying. "An ambitious young man like you always likes to be in the fight, or should I say in at the kill?"

There was a murmur of agreement from the Corporal, then Lord Rawthorne went on:

"Never mind, I am sure you will not lose any priority through being left behind, and I will certainly tell the Captain and other superior officials that you have performed your duties in an exemplary manner."

"Thank you, Lord Sahib."

"When do you expect Captain Sleeman back?"

"I do not know, Lord Sahib."

"How long will it take him to reach the place he has gone?"

"It is not very far, Lord Sahib."

"Yes, of course! I was told the name. Now let me think—I find Indian places are rather difficult to remember."

"Selopa, Lord Sahib."

"Yes, yes, of course. How stupid of me. Selopa! Well, I shall wait with impatience for his return, as I am sure you will, Corporal."

"Yes, Lord Sahib."

"Good-night, Corporal."

"Good-night, Lord Sahib."

Brucena held her breath.

She realised that Lord Rawthorne had got the information he required from the Corporal, and it was information that she herself did not know.

Selopa. That was where Iain had gone. But why was Lord Rawthorne so interested?

It seemed to her so strange that her mind was racing, trying to solve a puzzle which she knew instinctively was of importance.

She went back to her room to find her maid waiting.

"I did not expect you to come to bed so early, Mem Sahib," she said apologetically, "or I would have been waiting for you."

"It is all right," Brucena said. "I am not quite ready to undress. Will you fetch Nasir to me? I want to speak to him immediately."

"I fetch him, Mem Sahib."

The maid disappeared and Brucena waited.

A few seconds later Nasir came to the door and she told him to come in.

He was a small, wiry little man and she knew that Cousin William thought him to be very intelligent.

"Listen, Nasir," Brucena said, "I want you to find out something, and be very careful so that no-one realises what you are about."

She saw by the expression in his eyes that Nasir was alert and attentive.

"I have a feeling, although I may be wrong," Brucena continued, "that the Lord Sahib, Lord Rawthorne, may despatch a messenger from here tonight on an errand. If he does, he will send one of his men secretly and with the intention that none of us shall know that he has gone."

She paused before she added:

"That must not happen, Nasir."

"I will be watching, Mem Sahib."

"You will be able to do that?"

"Yes, Mem Sahib."

"If any of Lord Rawthorne's servants or one of the soldiers who came with him from Gwalior should leave, you must come and tell me at once . . . do you understand?"

"Yes, Mem Sahib."

"Just in case there is any gossip," Brucena went on, "tell anyone who is interested that I sent for you because I wanted to talk about Azim."

"No-one will question me, Mem Sahib," Nasir said. "But if they ask, that is what I tell them."

"Thank you, Nasir. I know I can trust you, but please, come and wake me if anybody leaves the bungalow."

"I will do that, Mem Sahib."

Nasir salaamed and left the room, and Brucena allowed her maid to help her undress, then she got into bed.

She might be mistaken, she thought as she lay back against her pillows, but the suspicions that she had felt after hearing Lord Rawthorne speak to the Corporal seemed to grow and grow.

Now they were like a cloud, dark and menacing, not to her but to Iain.

Yet she told herself that she was being very foolish. Surely Lord Rawthorne would not harm Iain. Could he be unsporting enough to contemplate anything underhanded just because he desired her?

Yet, he had said with an undeniable determination: "You will marry me!" and added a moment later that he would do anything to prevent her marriage to Iain.

What could he do?

She could not believe that the tentative suspicions already in her mind were not just fantasies, but they were there, however hard she tried to sweep them away.

She must have dozed a little before she heard her door open and instantly sat up in bed.

Nasir moved across the room so silently that he was beside her without her hearing a single footfall.

Then in a whisper he said:

"You right, Mem Sahib, one of the Lord Sahib's personal servants is saddling a horse."

"Then we must leave too," Brucena said quickly. "We have to warn Captain Sleeman and Major Huntley. Do you understand?"

"We, Mem Sahib?"

"You and I, Nasir. As soon as this man has left, saddle two horses. Wait a little way down the drive, behind the shrubs. You know the way to Selopa?"

"Yes, Mem Sahib."

"And you know where we will find the Captain Sahib?"

"Yes, Mem Sahib."

"Then hurry!"

Nasir left the room as silently as he had entered it and Brucena began to dress.

She put on her lightest riding-habit and her boots; then, carrying her broad-brimmed hat in her hand, she crept along the passage to Amelie's room.

She did not knock but opened the door quietly. As she did, Amelie asked:

"Who is it?"

"It is Brucena."

Amelia sat up against her pillows.

"What is it, dearest?"

Brucena went close to her before she spoke. The moonlight shining through the curtains over the window made it easy to see the way.

"I have to go to warn Cousin William and Iain that they are in danger," she said. "I think, although I am not certain, that a man has been sent to alert the Thugs they are seeking. They might in consequence take them off their guard and kill them. I have to tell them, Amelie, what is happening!"

"*Ma cherie,* how do you know this? How is it possible?" Amelie began.

"There is no time to tell you," Brucena said, "but I promise there is every reason for me to be afraid. Now listen, and this is vitally important. Lord Rawthorne must not know that I have left the Villa."

"But—why? How is he concerned in this?"

"He is very much concerned with it, at least I think so," Brucena replied. "So tomorrow, Amelie, you must say that I am unwell, that I have a fever. Make my maid pretend that I am ill in bed. Be careful to send my food in. She can throw it away somehow, but do not let anyone else in the whole house suspect that I have left."

Any other woman would have agreed but protested, but Amelie had not been married to William Sleeman without learning to be prepared for any sort of emergency and to ask few questions.

"Who is going with you?"

"Nasir," Brucena replied.

"You will be safe with him. I only hope William will not be angry that I am letting you go."

Brucena smiled as she bent to kiss Amelie's cheek.

"You would not be able to stop me," she said, "and I will be back as soon as I can."

She left the room by climbing over the side of the verandah, to find Nasir down the drive, holding two horses behind a high, concealing bank of shrubs.

He helped her into the saddle without speaking and they rode off, moving slowly over the soft ground so that their horses' hoofs would not be heard. Only when they were clear of the bungalow and out in the open countryside did their pace quicken.

The moonlight turned everything to silver and made the way as clear as if it were daytime.

For the first time Brucena felt a sudden exhilaration sweep through her.

She was helping Iain, and she knew that her love for him and his for her would enable her to

save him and to prevent the destruction of his and
Cousin William's plans.

Afterwards, Brucena wondered at the manner in
which Nasir never faltered and they hardly checked
their horses from the moment they started until they
reached their destination.

They had galloped a long way before Brucena
asked:

"How far is Selopa, Nasir?"

"Not far, way we travel," he answered.

Brucena looked at him, waiting for an explanation, and he said:

"Captain Sahib go by main road so not attract
attention, just like ordinary patrol, inspection of
prison, meet District Officers. No hurry, no-one think
anything strange."

"Of course, I understand," Brucena replied, and
they hurried on.

She had the feeling that Nasir was taking her
through the wildest, most uninhabited part of the
country, for they seldom crossed a road and there
were few little villages.

In fact, they moved through an empty, moonlit
world that she would have found very beautiful if she
had not been driven by an urgency that made her
unable to think of anything except that Iain was in
danger.

Supposing she was too late? Supposing the man
that Lord Rawthorne had sent—she was sure he had
sent him to the Thugs—got there before she did and
they took Cousin William and Iain by surprise?

She had no idea exactly how many soldiers they
had with them, but she remembered with a shudder
the story of how Cousin William had at one time
captured a gang of over three hundred Thugs con-
gregated in one place.

If there were that many now, what chance
would they have?

On and on they galloped, Nasir leading the way,

the horses responding to everything they asked of
them, and Brucena was glad that Cousin William
bought good horse-flesh.

It was his one extravagance and she knew that
in this instance it was proving its worth.

At last, after they had ridden for what seemed
a very long time, Nasir drew in his reins and proceeded a little more slowly.

He was looking about him and Brucena guessed
without asking questions that he was searching for a
place where Cousin William and Iain would have
camped for the night.

She tried to imagine what their plan would have
been.

Surely it would be one of surprise, but how were
they likely to surprise Thugs in the act of strangling
travellers if they rode up to them as Cavalrymen,
with the irregulars carrying their lances?

'Perhaps I have made a fool of myself,' Brucena
thought suddenly and despairingly. 'He may in fact
be sleeping in a Barracks somewhere, having been
entertained in the Officers' Mess.'

But she knew in her heart that that was unlikely,
and even as she puzzled, Nasir suddenly dismounted
and signalled for her to do the same.

He did not speak, and Brucena remembered
that voices carried at night and were therefore likely
to reveal their whereabouts.

She slipped from her saddle and followed Nasir,
who was leading his horse into a thicket of trees.

When she joined him she found that he was
tying the reins to a tree-trunk and she did the same
with hers.

Nasir put his fingers to his lips, then started to
move ahead. Brucena, lifting the skirt of her habit,
followed him, not asking where they were going but
trying to move as silently as he was doing, knowing
that her heart was beating unaccountably quickly.

They began to descend through a wood which had a thick undergrowth beneath the trees. It forced them to move slowly, until suddenly below them Brucena saw a large party of travellers camped for the night.

There were horses with their legs hobbled so that they could not move away, a camel was squatting on the ground with its head held high, and all round it appeared to be a large number of anonymous bundles that she knew were men covered with blankets and cloaks.

A little apart and nearer to the trees there were two tents, small and low.

They were the type used by travellers of a certain class who felt themselves too important to sleep beside their men but were not important enough to have the large, imposing tents erected for rich merchants or Sahibs.

Nasir stood for some time without moving; then, dropping to his knees, he started to crawl towards the tents. He signalled to her to follow him and she crouched down.

She wanted to ask what he was doing.

The people below them were travellers, certainly not soldiers.

Then it suddenly struck her that if Cousin William and Iain intended to catch the Thugs red-handed, they might present themselves as victims. They would be the travellers, they would be the baited trap!

She felt her heart give a lurch of fear. Then as Nasir went on crawling downhill with a quietness and stealth which came from long experience, she knew how careful she must be not to be heard.

She felt as if every leaf on which she knelt made a crack like a rifle-shot and every twig snapped like the roar of a cannon.

Then almost before she realised it they were within a few feet of the tents.

Nasir turned his head and held up his hand. It was a signal, she guessed, for her to stay where she was.

He realised that she understood, and slowly, very slowly, he crept forward and lifted the bottom of the tent in front of him.

The moonlight was somewhat obscured by the branches of the trees, and yet Brucena saw that as sinuously as a snake he crept into the tent, and now she was alone.

She listened for the sound of voices but could hear nothing.

Then she began to wonder frantically whether he had gone to the wrong place, and perhaps, suspected of being a thief, he had been killed!

Then she saw his face appear from under the tent. He smiled at her and beckoned.

As she moved forward he crept towards the other tent, again lifting the bottom sheet to vanish inside it.

Frightened but obedient, Brucena crawled the short distance from the undergrowth to the tent. As she reached it, a hand came out towards her, and her heart seemed to turn three somersaults.

It was Iain's hand. He pulled her inside and a second later she was in his arms.

Then he was kissing her until she forgot everything except that she was with him again, and she knew she need not be afraid because she was against his heart.

He released her lips, and in a voice so low that she had to strain her ears to hear it, he asked:

"How could you be so incredibly brave to come to warn me?"

She felt, as he spoke, that his kisses had taken everything from her mind except the wonder of him.

Then, as quietly as he had spoken, she began to explain what she had overheard and what she suspected.

"It was very wonderful of you, my darling. But I do not want you here in danger. And if there is time, I think Nasir should take you away again."

"No, no!" Brucena whispered. "I will not leave."

She put her arms round his neck, saying:

"I am not afraid now that I am with you. I am only afraid when you are not there."

"I think you should go back," Iain said, "but your cousin must decide. Nasir is telling him now why you have come."

As he spoke, there was a sudden cry like a word of command, followed by a pandemonium of noise. In an instant Iain had pulled open the flap in the front of his tent and moved outside.

Brucena gave a little cry which was strangled in her throat.

Then she was alone, listening to terrifying sounds which were, she knew, those of life or death.

But for whom?

Chapter Seven

"Good-bye, dearest Amelie. I cannot thank you enough for all you have done for me."

"I shall miss you terribly," Amelie replied, "as William will miss Iain, but we know how happy you both will be."

As the two women embraced inside the railway-carriage, William Sleeman, standing on the platform, held out his hand to Iain Huntley.

"There is no need for me to tell you to take care of Brucena," he said, "and although things will not be the same here without you, I know that you have a great future ahead of you."

"If I have, I owe it all to you," Iain replied, "and may I say in all sincerity that I have never enjoyed anything more than the years we have been to-gether."

"At least we have a record of success behind us," William Sleeman replied. "There is little to do now except mop up the few things that remain. But I am quite certain the Thugs will have lost heart."

Inside the carriage, Brucena picked up her wedding-bouquet, which had been laid on the seat, and pressed it into Amelie's hands.

"In case I am not able to give you flowers when your baby arrives," she said, "I would like to feel

145

that these were the first that he or she will ever receive."

Amelie laughed a little tremulously.

"It is a sweet thought," she said, "and I shall press many of these flowers in a scrap-book so that I can show them to my child when he is grown up."

Both women smiled shyly as if they felt a little embarrassed at being so sentimental.

Then William Sleeman said from the door:

"The guard is asking if he can start the train, Amelie, and unless you want to leave with the honey-moon-couple, I suggest you finish your good-byes!"

Amelie kissed Brucena once more.

"You look lovely, dearest," she said, "and whatever you may say, I know it will not be many years before you live in a Government House of your own and are addressed as 'My Lady.'"

Because it was now such an old joke, Brucena did not protest. She only laughed, and as Amelie was helped out of the carriage, she kissed her cousin.

"Good-bye, Cousin William," she said. "'Thank you' is a most inadequate phrase. I only know, as I felt when I arrived in India, that it is the most exciting, marvellous country in the whole world."

She glanced at her husband as she spoke, and added:

"Especially as it gave me Iain."

William turned to the guard who was hovering near them.

"You have my permission," he said, "to start the train."

"Thank you, Captain Sahib," the guard replied, and, putting his whistle into his mouth, he started to unfurl his flag.

The Sepoys were holding back the excited crowds who were watching Brucena and Iain's departure.

A bride and bridegroom in any country are always an attraction, and Brucena's going-away gown, of pale pink with a bonnet trimmed with ribbons

of the same colour, had evoked cries of delight from
the Indian women in their colourful saris.

There was a burst of steam from the engine,
and as Iain stepped into the carriage and shut the
door and their servants in the next compartment shut
theirs, a cheer went up from all those who were
watching.

As the train moved away from the platform,
Brucena leant out the window with a suspicion of
tears in her eyes as she waved good-bye to Cousin
William and Amelie.

Only as the wheels quickened and the smoke
began to obscure their view did Iain draw her into
the carriage and shut the window.

Then as she stood looking at him, swaying a
little with the movement of the train, he drew her
into his arms and kissed her.

It was not a long kiss, because as they gathered
speed they were forced to sit down, but it brought
the colour to Brucena's cheeks and a light to her eyes.

"We are married!" she said in a low voice. "We
are . . . really married!"

"Were you afraid something would stop us at
the last minute?" Iain asked.

"I am never sure of anything where you are
concerned," she replied. "How could I ever have
guessed, when I was so afraid of what your next
exploit with Cousin William might be, that you would
be offered this wonderful position on the Governor-
General's staff?"

"You can thank your cousin for that," Iain replied. "His report was so glowing that no Governor-
General, especially Lord William Bentinck, who was
particularly interested in our achievements, could
have ignored it."

"Whatever Cousin William said, I am sure none
of it was exaggerated."

Iain smiled and put his arms round her as he
said:

"I am afraid, darling, that you are somewhat prejudiced in my favour, but that is exactly how I want it to be."

With his free hand he undid the ribbons that were tied under her chin, took off her bonnet, and threw it on an empty seat.

Then when she thought he was about to kiss her, he sat looking at her until he said quietly:

"I do not believe that anyone can be so beautiful. Actually, I thought that when we first met in a railway-carriage."

"We started our acquaintanceship in one, and now we are starting our marriage in one!" Brucena cried. "I feel that special quirk of fate has a lesson somewhere, but I am not quite certain what it means."

"It means that I love you and you are my wife," Iain said. "But because you are so beautiful, I am not certain that I have been wise in accepting a position on the Governor-General's staff."

Brucena looked at him enquiringly and he explained:

"If I catch you looking at another man or listening to the compliments you will inevitably receive, I swear I will take you back to Saugor and we will stay there for the rest of our lives!"

"It would not matter to me where we were as long as I was with you," Brucena replied.

Then, because there was a very moving note of sincerity in her voice, Iain kissed her and it was impossible to say any more.

*　　*　　*

Only later did Brucena have time to think of how her life had changed overnight, and not only because she had married Iain.

She was to learn how important her part had been in riding with Nasir to Selopa to warn Cousin William of Lord Rawthorne's treachery.

She had been right in suspecting that he intended to alert the Thugs whom they were out to capture.

Worse than that, he had told his messenger to inform the Thugs that they must fight for their lives, whoever they destroyed in the process.

It had been a direct invitation to kill, and Brucena felt guilty that it was in a way her fault that he had stooped to such a disgraceful action in order to destroy the man she wanted to marry.

"How could he behave in such a criminal manner?" she had cried when she was told of Lord Rawthorne's directions.

She had been appalled that any man, especially an English nobleman, should commit what really amounted to cold-blooded murder.

Iain had put his arm round her.

"I think, my darling," he said, "we have to be generous and accept that his passion for you destroyed his balance and his common sense."

"I can think of more unpleasant words to describe his behaviour," William Sleeman had said drily.

"So can I," Iain admitted, but quite frankly, I think there is no point in saying so."

Brucena looked from one man to the other in perplexity.

"Are you telling me that you are going to let Lord Rawthorne get away with this?" she asked. "Surely you will tell the Governor-General, or at least you must challenge him to give you an explanation?"

William Sleeman was silent for a moment, then he said:

"No. Iain is right, Brucena. Nothing can be gained by making a scandal, and it is far more dignified for us to pretend that we had no idea he was involved in any way in what, thanks to you, my dear, was a most successful operation."

"You mean ... if I had not got there ... before Lord Rawthorne's man ..."

"There might have been a very different story to tell," Iain said, as if he wished to prevent her from saying any more. "As you know, Nasir told your cousin why you had come, and he gave the arranged signal to seize the Thugs before they were ready to start work on us."

However, Brucena found there was a great deal more to it than that.

By means of espionage in Gwalior, Iain had learnt that the two remaining leaders of the Thugs in their Province had arranged a meeting on one of the special days dedicated to Kali.

He had discovered that this meeting was to take place in a grove that had been notorious for generations as a haunt of the Thugs, a *bele*, or place of strangulation.

In that particular place where Brucena had joined them, for several centuries, hundreds, perhaps thousands, of innocent travellers had been murdered.

There had been a large market in Selopa and the Thug leaders knew that because the *bele* was at a convenient point on the road outside the town, a party of travellers would be bound to stop there to rest before their journey home the next day.

The Thugs would hope for a large party and would be ready to demonstrate their well-tried technique with a yellow silken noose.

When the victims were dead, they would cut the bodies about with ritual gashes and bury them under the trees, thus making their obeisance to their goddess by means of a human sacrifice, for which they would obtain great merit.

This success would be reported to all the Thugs who were left in the vicinity and would re-establish their power, which had been considerably reduced by William Sleeman's suppression of so many followers of their cult.

It had been an act of defiance, an act which might have undone a great deal of the good work that had been achieved in the last two years.

What was more, had Lord Rawthorne's messenger arrived before Brucena and managed to convey his information to the leader of the Thugs without William Sleeman or Iain Huntley being aware of it, their victory might easily have been a tragic defeat.

The Thugs would have had two alternatives—one, to disappear; the other, to start strangling their supposed fellow-travellers before Sleeman's disguised men were ready for them.

As it was, they were taken entirely by surprise, having, owing to the cleverness of William Sleeman and Iain, already been deceived into believing that the party they had joined in the *bele* were bona fide travellers.

Because he felt it was only fair that Brucena should understand exactly what had happened, Cousin William had told her how before they reached Selopa they had left their horses in a place of concealment which had already been arranged.

There they had changed from their uniforms into garments worn by the local farmers of another part of the country.

Then, carrying market-produce for sale, they had infiltrated into the town, bargaining for their wares and meeting again only at the end of the day.

Bringing a camel which Iain had acquired and several donkeys, they had set off along the road, talking of how much money they had made and boasting that it had been an exceedingly successful day's marketing.

William Sleeman had drilled his men so well that from the moment they discarded their uniforms, they played their parts whether they thought anyone was listening or not.

For nearly three years he had taught them that a careless word, a moment off their guard, might result not only in their own deaths but the deaths of their comrades.

When they reached the chosen *bele* they argued for some time as to whether they should camp there for the night or go on farther.

There appeared to be nobody about, but there were bushes in which men could have concealed themselves, and the trees were thick.

They were still talking when what looked like a party of travellers, a large one, joined them. These, they were well aware, were the Thugs.

"You are camping here?" one of them asked.

"We are trying to make up our minds," Iain replied in fluent Urdu.

"There is room for us both," the Thug said.

"We are still a long way from home."

"We understand if you wish to proceed," the Thug replied.

A well-trained chorus of voices asserted that they were tired and could go no farther, and finally, after a great deal more argument, which Indians always enjoy, they agreed that they would all camp together.

Another, smaller party of Thugs joined them, and William Sleeman and Iain noticed that after they had sat for a little while talking and exchanging stories, individuals attached themselves in a friendly manner to different men of their own party.

When finally they began to make preparations to sleep, the Thugs lay down beside their new-found companions.

Only William and Iain insisted on having tents to themselves, and this was quite understandable because they were dressed as richer and more important merchants.

They had made it obvious that quite a number of the travellers were in their employment and also that they owned the camel.

William Sleeman's instructions had been not to start the fight, if that was what it was to be, too soon.

He wanted to be quite sure that all the Thugs belonging to each leader were present, and he also planned, where possible, to catch them with a yellow scarf in their hands.

It would be enough to bring them to justice if they merely had a yellow scarf concealed about their person.

At the same time, for the sentence to be as heavy as he wanted it to be, he had to catch a Thug in the act of committing murder, which resulted in his either being hanged or given a life-sentence.

However, when he learnt from Nasir that the Thugs were to be warned that they had been tricked, there was no time to be lost.

Taken completely by surprise, none of the Thugs tried to escape, but fought for their lives, and many died doing so.

The rest were taken to Saugor to the prison, and the following week the two leaders and the most competent of the men were condemned to be hanged.

The rest were branded, and the fact that such a large operation had been brought off without a single Thug escaping had such a startling effect on the local population that William Sleeman had said triumphantly:

"This is practically, if not completely, the end of my mission!"

Brucena had given a cry of sheer delight, and William's report had been carried post-haste to the Governor-General.

The immediate result was that Iain Huntley was offered a position on Lord William Bentinck's staff.

It had been, he thought when he received it,

almost an answer to a prayer, for while he wanted
to marry Brucena immediately, there was some
difficulty in finding a bungalow in the neighbourhood
of Saugor that he thought was good enough for her.

He also had the feeling that after all she had
been through she would find it difficult not to be
increasingly anxious if he was away from her for
even one night.

She would put on a brave face, he knew that
already. At the same time, it was not usual for an
Englishwoman, even in India, to suffer as she had
suffered when he had been left behind in Gwalior,
and certainly not to be actually on the spot in a
fight which resulted in the deaths of a large number
of those involved.

She had been afraid, Iain knew, only for him.

When finally the Thugs who had survived were
whining miserably for mercy as they were tied up
by the jubilant Sepoys, he had gone into his tent
to find Brucena crouched on the ground, her hands
clasped together and her lips moving in prayer.

He would have taken her in his arms, but he
realised that his native garments were stained with
blood from the sword-thrusts he had made at the
Thugs, who had fought back with the knives with
which they mutilated their victims.

Instead he merely put out his hand and said
quietly:

"It is all over, my darling, and now we can go
home."

After that, although he had not said so, he had
almost desperately wanted to offer Brucena a different sort of life, even though he knew that he would
never be happy anywhere other than in India.

The Governor-General's invitation had therefore
been not only opportune but very exciting.

Iain knew it was not only an immediate advance-
ment but the first step on the ladder which led
eventually to becoming a Resident, and, if one was

exceptionally lucky or clever, after that, to Lieutenant-Governor of a Province.

To Brucena the only thing that mattered was that they could be married before Iain left for Calcutta.

"You will not ... go without me?" she had asked anxiously.

"Do you imagine I would leave you behind?" he enquired.

There had been all the excitement of arranging the wedding and of providing herself, in a few days, with a wedding-dress in which she hoped Iain would think her beautiful.

Fortunately, Amelie had an evening-gown which had arrived from her father as a present, but because she had lost her figure it had been impossible for her to wear it.

"You must keep it until after the baby has arrived," Brucena protested.

Amelie laughed.

"I will get Papa to send me another one. Besides, what is more important than that you should be a beautiful bride for Iain? Thank goodness I have some lace which we can easily make into a veil."

One thing was certain—the little Church in Saugor had never seen a more beautiful bride, and when Brucena had walked up the aisle on Cousin William's arm, she had known by the expression in Iain's eyes that she was everything he wanted her to be.

The Service had been to Brucena very moving and she had prayed that she would make Iain happy.

She had known, because they were so closely attuned, that he was praying for the same thing.

When they had signed the Marriage-Register in the Vestry and he had raised her veil in a symbolic gesture and kissed her, she had known that it was a kiss of dedication and that he gave her his heart and soul.

After toasts had been drunk at the bungalow, Brucena had to change hurriedly into her going-away gown if they were not to miss the train.

It was to be a strange honeymoon because they would be travelling right across India to Calcutta.

Although they were starting off in a train, their journey could entail travelling in a dozen different ways.

There were very few railways as yet in India, although the British were busy constructing lines between the most important towns.

The first day they would be able to cover only about thirty miles by train. Then they were to stay in a bungalow which had been lent them, and leave two days later by road for the next stop.

To Brucena the whole idea was an enchantment which left her breathless with excitement.

It was getting late when the train stopped at the small station where they were to leave it.

William Sleeman's friends who had lent them their bungalow were in Bombay, but their servants had brought a carriage to the station, and they collected their luggage from the guard's van and their other belongings from the carriage.

They drove in the cool of the evening through a wooded countryside to a white bungalow built on the side of a small lake. It was surrounded with flowers and Brucena gave a cry of delight when she saw it.

Then as the servants brought them cool drinks, they stood side by side on the verandah. There was the glory of the sunset, dyeing the lake and the long sandbanks with gold.

Every tree and cane-brake became the colour of a warm, glowing apricot, a prelude to the swift opal twilight.

"It is so lovely," Brucena murmured.

"And so are you, my darling," Iain replied, and

there was a note in his voice that made her heart beat tumultuously in her breast.

When Brucena went to her bedroom a little later, she found it attractive and very comfortable. The large bedstead in the centre of it, draped with white mosquito-curtains, looked like an ancient galleon and made her blush.

She stood for a moment, thinking that it was the first "home" that she and Iain would have together and therefore she must somehow make it personal.

She had already thought of this amidst the excitement of planning her wedding, and in her luggage packed especially for use on the journey she had included a miniature of her mother and a beautifully embroidered bed-cover.

This Amelie had made of muslin ribbon and lace, and it had been intended, she said, as a Christmas-present for someone in Mauritius.

Instead, she had given it to Brucena and with it there was a little lace pillow with love-knots in each of its four corners.

When Brucena had arranged these on the bedspread, she felt it gave the room a touch that was a part of herself.

She also had with her a present that she thought was more precious than anything else she had received: the carved whistle that Azim had given her just before they left.

She knew it was his most treasured possession and she therefore must not hurt him by refusing it.

As she laid it beside her mother's portrait, she told herself that she would keep it all her life and perhaps one day tell her children of how it came to be hers.

She looked round her with a little sigh of satisfaction. Then, because she thought Iain would be waiting for her, she let the Indian maid help her change into her prettiest evening-gown. As she had no jewellery, she arranged a white orchid in her hair.

There was an obvious look of admiration and love in his eyes when she went into the Sitting-Room to find that he had changed into the evening-dress of the Bengal Lancers.

"Now I know why I have waited for half-a-century," he said, "but it has been worth it!"

"Have I been very long?" Brucena asked. "I wanted to look pretty for you ... tonight."

" 'Pretty' is a very inadequate word to describe you, my lovely one," he replied.

The servants were waiting to serve their dinner and so there was no chance for him to kiss her. Yet as they sat opposite each other Brucena felt she was close in his arms, and their eyes said all the things their lips could not say.

What they ate or drank she had no idea. She knew only that she was living in an enchanted world where there were only two people, Iain and herself.

When they went back into the Sitting-Room, the oil-lamps filled it with a soft golden light while outside the stars covered the heavens with a jewel-like brilliance.

There were so many things to talk about, so many things she wanted to know which only Iain could tell her, and the time slipped by.

When finally she realised it was getting late, Brucena found her voice dying away and she knew by the expression on Iain's face that there was no more need for conversation.

He put out his hands and drew her to her feet.

"It is time you went to bed, my precious one," he said, "and I told your maid not to wait on you, as I want us to be alone."

"That ... is what I want ... too," Brucena wanted to say, but she felt shy.

Instead, she hid her face against his neck.

He kissed her hair, then with his arms round her he drew her across the passage and into the bedroom.

Here there was only one little oil-lamp burning beside the bed.

It shone on the lace cover and on the small lace pillow perched bravely on the large white linen one.

There was a smile on Iain's lips as he looked at his wife. Then he took the white orchid from Brucena's hair and pulled out the pins so that it fell over her shoulders in a golden cloud.

"That is how I saw you the night you were so frightened, when you ran into me in the passage," he said. "Although you were terror-struck, I thought no woman could look more beautiful or be so soft and sweet and enchanting in every way."

"You ... kissed me," Brucena said, "without asking if ... you might do so."

"It was very remiss of me," he said, with laughter in his voice, "but I obeyed an uncontrollable impulse which I have never regretted."

"I have ... never regretted it ... either," Brucena whispered, "but I have often wondered if I had not been so frightened at that particular moment ... whether you would have kissed me ... or have been sure that you ... loved me."

"I was sure of myself but not of you," he answered. "I thought perhaps you still hated me."

"I loved you ... although I did not ... know it."

"And now?"

"I love you with all my heart!"

"That is what I want you to say," he answered.

Then as his lips met hers she felt him undoing the buttons at the back of her gown. . . .

*   *   *

Later, very much later, when there was only the music of the night and the beat of Iain's heart, Brucena asked:

"Is it ... possible to be so ... happy and not ... die of the wonder of it?"

"You are very much alive, my precious one," Iain said, drawing her closer and kissing her fore-head. "Have I really made you happy?"

"So happy that I am ... afraid."

"Afraid?" he questioned.

"That I shall wake up and find it is all a dream! ... How can all this be real?"

"It is real, that I promise you."

"Everything that has happened to us is just like a story in a book," Brucena said. "First, that you should be so brave and so wonderful! Then that you should love me, and lastly that we should be married. Oh, Iain, tell me it is true!"

He laughed gently and his lips moved over the softness of her skin.

"I will keep proving my love," he said, "until you are absolutely convinced in every corner of your mind that you are mine, completely and absolutely mine! The story of our love is as true as it is true that we are in India and the whole great Continent is ours."

"Supposing you become too ... grand and I ... lose you?"

"Do you think that is likely?" he asked. "My darling, you forget that one of the reasons I am grander than I was last month is entirely due to you."

His mouth moved along her eye-lids before he continued:

"They say a successful man always has a woman behind him, pushing him up the ladder of success, and that is what you have done."

"I am glad ... so very ... very glad."

Iain turned her face up to his.

"We are neither of us going to get so grand," he said, "that we grow away from each other or the people who matter. There will always be Azims in

India who will need our help and support. There
will aways be wrongs to be righted and Thugs in
one form or another to be suppressed."

"You will let me ... help you?" Brucena asked
quickly.

"I am not only going to let you, but I insist
upon it," Iain replied. "Your quickness of thought
and your presence of mind has saved me already
and will, I know, save me again."

"I do not ... want to think of you being in ...
danger."

"It may play a small part in our lives," he said
seriously, "but if you use that special instinct of yours,
sweet darling, I would trust you in any emergency."

"Oh, Iain, I am glad ... so very, very glad,"
Brucena cried. "I want to be the right ... sort of
wife for you. I want to feel that you can rely on
me."

"I know I can do that," he answered.

"Amelie is the right sort of wife for Cousin William. At first I could not understand why she did
not fuss and fume every time he left her. Then I
clearly knew why, when I was waiting for you the
other night in that horrible little tent."

"Why?" Iain asked.

"Amelie believes implicitly," Brucena answered,
"in William and in God, and it makes her sure that
whatever danger he is in, he will come back to
her."

She drew a deep breath.

"I will do the same: I will believe in you ... my
marvellous husband, and ... in God."

Iain held her very close against him. Then he
said in a voice that told her he was deeply moved:

"Could any woman be more wonderful? I adore
you for the things you say to me, for your thoughts
that are like stars shining in the darkness. I also find
your softness and your beauty irresistible, because
every perfect part of you belongs to me."

"I am . . . yours . . . all yours."

She spoke with a note of passion in her voice because Iain's hand was touching her and she felt the little fire that he had awakened in her earlier rising again in her breast.

As if he felt it too, he laid her gently against the pillows so that she was on her back, looking up at him.

In the flickering light of the oil-lamp he could see her eyes, wide, excited, and, he thought, with a little touch of fire in their depths.

His hand became more insistent and Brucena raised her lips to his, wanting him to kiss her, wanting the closeness which she knew he wanted too.

"You have bewitched me!" Iain said.

Then his lips were on her lips and his heart was beating against her heart!

They were no longer two people but one, and there was no more darkness but only the divine love which casts out fear.

ABOUT THE AUTHOR

BARBARA CARTLAND, the world's most famous romantic novelist, who is also an historian, playwright, lecturer, political speaker and television personality, has now written over 200 books.

She has also had many historical works published and has written four autobiographies as well as the biographies of her mother and that of her brother Ronald Cartland, who was the first Member of Parliament to be killed in the last war. This book has a preface by Sir Winston Churchill.

Barbara Cartland has sold 100 million books over the world, more than half of these in the U.S.A. She broke the world record in 1975 by writing twenty books, and her own record in 1976 with twenty-one. In addition, her album of love songs has just been published, sung with the Royal Philharmonic Orchestra.

In private life, Barbara Cartland, who is a Dame of the Order of St. John of Jerusalem, has fought for better conditions and salaries for Midwives and Nurses. As President of the Royal College of Midwives (Hertfordshire Branch), she has been invested with the first Badge of Office ever given in Great Britain, which was subscribed to by the Midwives themselves. She has also championed the cause for old people and founded the first Romany Gypsy Camp in the world.

Barbara Cartland is deeply interested in Vitamin Therapy and is President of the British National Association for Health.